Jesus Coyote

Published by Raw Dog Screaming Press
Hyattsville, MD

First Paperback Edition

Cover photograph & design: Norman Conquest
Book design: Jennifer Barnes
Author photo: Gayle Luque

Printed in the United States of America

ISBN 978-1-933293-63-9

Library of Congress Control Number: 2008922036

www.rawdogscreaming.com

Critical Response to Harold Jaffe's Fiction & "Docufiction"

Beyond the Techno-Cave: A Guerrilla Writer's Guide to Post-Millennial Culture "Harold Jaffe's book is a work of non-fiction. Yet it is a work of such range and erudition that it defies simple categories." —*The Brooklyn Rail*

Terror-Dot-Gov "Everywhere in Terror-dot-Gov is exemplary skill, faultless tonality. And courage, don't forget courage." —*Daniel Berrigan, SJ*

15 Serial Killers "With this latest salvo of guerrilla writing, Harold Jaffe explodes the very social, political, and narrative structures supporting capitalist culture's illusory edifices, further cementing his reputation as one of our finest literary terrorists/freedom fighters." —*Paradoxa*

False Positive "These short treats transform 15 news vignettes into gruesomely interesting oddities. Jaffe is a master at illuminating our culture's most evasive grotesqueries." —*San Francisco Chronicle*

Sex for the Millennium "Something's going on here, low-key, cool, and disturbing. These subtle displacements of desire fix to your memory, and, with their humor and pathos, gnaw there a long time." —*Samuel R. Delany*

Straight Razor "As technically outrageous and emotionally intense as a madman's shotgun held to the temple of contemporary culture. [Jaffe's 12 stories] succeed terrifically." —*Review of Contemporary Fiction*

Othello Blues "With multi-layered dialogue and descriptions as clipped and terse as stage directions, Jaffe uses his science fiction setting to hold a satirist's funhouse mirror to our own contemporary world, showing us the rich grown richer, the poor poorer, and the powerful…indifferent to the misery around them, a world to which the blues is an all too appropriate response." —*Rain Taxi*

Eros Anti-Eros "Jaffe's fictions are a wonder of deadpan humor, biting wit, and visual beauty. No recent fiction has gripped me with such force and immediacy." —*Marianne Hauser*

Madonna and Other Spectacles "Crackling with rage and black laughter, these fictions wrench themselves out of the grimmest facts: genocide, nuclear devastation, black poverty, corporate murder. [This is] a collection that confronts terror in street language and redoubles its impact." —*Publisher's Weekly*

Beasts "Jaffe's convincing portraits of the dispossessed are moving, insightful glimpses of the human spirit under stress." —*The New York Times Book Review*

Dos Indios "Told with the simplicity of a folk tale, this spiritual journey of a Peruvian flute player is a beautiful and moving story." —*Newsday*

Books by Harold Jaffe

Jesus Coyote (novel)

Beyond the Techno-Cave: A Guerrilla Writer's Guide to Post-Millennial Culture (non-fiction)

Terror-Dot-Gov (docufictions; visuals by Katana Blue)

15 Serial Killers (docufictions; visuals by Joel Lipman)

False Positive (docufictions)

Sex for the Millennium (extreme tales)

Straight Razor (fictions; visuals by Norman Conquest)

Othello Blues (novel)

Eros Anti-Eros (fictions)

Madonna and Other Spectacles (fictions)

Beasts (fictions)

Dos Indios (novel)

Mourning Crazy Horse (fictions)

Mole's Pity (novel)

Acknowledgements

I'd like to thank Andy Koopmans, Gary Lain and Stephen-Paul Martin for reading and commenting on this novel in manuscript.

For C.M.

stayin' alive

The decisive blows are always struck left-handed
—Walter Benjamin

Author's note: Although the crucial murders in *Jesus Coyote* occur in August 1969, I have deliberately conflated the timeline so that selected events and concepts which in "real life" occurred *after* 1969 are included as if they had occurred *before* 1969.

Resemblances to the Charles Manson "family" saga are of course deliberate, but I have changed names and altered circumstances, since *Jesus Coyote* does not profess to be "factual."

Real Toads in Imaginary Gardens

Massacres

The mass murder in Joya Grove featuring the beautiful pregnant actress Naomi Self occurred on the night of 8 August 1969 and received massive, lurid front-page coverage, such as is customarily reserved for declarations of war or the toppling of world trade centers. The *LA Times*:

Blood Orgy in Hollywood Mansion

Movie Star, 4 Others, Brutally Slain

Satanism Hinted

The second series of murders, committed the following night, received this treatment:

Ritual Slayings Follow Killing of 5

Wealthy Bel Air Couple Stabbed and Mutilated

Blood Messages Smeared on Walls

The victims in the combined massacres were reportedly stabbed more than 270 times, and it was rumored that the beautiful actress's 8-month fetus was ripped from her womb.

Other rumors, no less lurid, made the rounds. In extraordinary circumstances, collective delirium will graft its ghastliest imaginings onto fact—which is already ghastly.

That same delirium impelled the California governor, a celebrated sportsperson, to jet home from his "guided safari" vacation in Tanzania without having fired a single shot at a rollicking wildebeest.

After a hectic all-night session with staff and advisers, the governor devised a "special" task force which combined the various expertise of the LAPD; LASO (LA County Sheriff's Office); FBI (since federal trespass was suspected); ATF; DEA; US Marshals Service; and the California National Guard.

Thus was launched the largest manhunt in LA history. But after nearly four months, with a media-agitated public clamoring for justice, the task force had accumulated numerous theories and no viable suspects.

The favored theory centered around illicit drugs. Each of the Joya Grove victims was reputed to be a heavy drug user, and the official speculation was that the victims, with the possible exceptions of Naomi Self and Phillip Morris heiress Kristin Barrett, were affiliated with the international drug cartel. This applied especially to Self's former lover, acclaimed "hairstylist to the stars" Don Fernando, and to Viktor Hus, Czech national and close friend of Self's notorious film director-husband, Jaroslav Hora.

One FBI official, requesting anonymity, labeled Hus "the chief conduit of MDMA [Ecstasy] from Israel and the Netherlands to the Pacific rim"; while Don Fernando was "*the*" supplier of Colombian A-grade cocaine and opiated Kabul hash to his movie star clients.

In the instance of the fifth victim, 19-year-old Billy Strayhorn, stabbed 27 times in his metallic green Karmann Ghia on the Joya Grove property, officials speculated that he was a drug courier in the process of collecting cash or delivering product.

As one well-heeled Brentwood doper put it: Immediately after the Joya Grove massacre, officially attributed to illicit drugs, one could imagine hearing ten thousand toilets flush throughout Hollywood and the opulent LA 'burbs.

The murders on the following night of the Bel Air couple, Giuseppe and Lena Gallo, also had a suspected connection with illicit drugs. Giuseppe "Mambo

Joe" Gallo, cousin to Joey Gallo of the New York crime syndicate, was a multimillionaire with strong ties to the Las Vegas Mafia and no visible means of support. His business card listed his profession as "impresario." Lena Gallo, his spouse, an ex-Vegas lounge singer, was reportedly a heavy coke user.

In each massacre the same weird, possibly satanic syllables **CRO** and **TOX** were scrawled in blood on the walls. No one professed to understand what these syllables signified. Nor could it be determined whether they were written by the same hand, because the crude block letters and all-over blood made an accurate assessment impossible.

At this early stage in the investigation the task force viewed the bloody scrawls as possible attempts to distract them from the actual motive: drug-related contract murders.

What if illicit drugs had nothing to do with the mass murders?

In that case, the task force held these alternate theories in reserve: Satanic thrill-killing; fame-wealth antagonism; Soviet-sponsored terrorism (film director Hora and his compatriot Hus were both anti-Communist Jews); and simple robbery, with an attempt to obscure the robbery by leaving selected valuables intact and "satanizing" the scene.

Whatever the actual motive, the intensive, far-flung investigation had almost nothing to show for four full months when three breaks occurred almost simultaneously. First Roxanne "Roxi" Bakramp, 21, an ex-pornographic supermodel and one of Jesus Coyote's most rabid acolytes, incarcerated since mid-September in the Sybil Brand Institute in LA on a seemingly unrelated charge, boasted of her involvement in the Self slayings to her cellmate, Luisa Alonzo, which Alonzo duly reported to the warden.

The fact is that since her arrest, Roxi Bakramp had repeatedly admitted her involvement, detailing and embroidering the massacre with a precision that only a participant (or madwoman) would possess, but Alonzo was unable to get the warden's attention until mid-November.

The second break occurred virtually at the same time. Elizabeth Ginzburg, 17, aka Li'l Bess, pregnant daughter of Dr. Ely Ginzburg, a prominent cosmetic surgeon from Rancho Santa Fe, California, evidently talked in her sleep in the presence of her mother, the socialite and cereal heiress Grace Nabisco-Ginzburg, who shook her daughter awake and extorted a full confession: Elizabeth was a member of the Coyote tribe; she smoked, snorted and swallowed all manner of illicit substances; had sex daily and indiscriminately; and had no clear idea who the father of her unborn child was, though suspected it was cult leader Coyote himself.

But the still bigger "confession" was that "Li'l Bess" had been involved, though only tangentially, she claimed, in the Self murders, masterminded, she said, by Jesus Coyote.

The Ginzburgs calculated that having their daughter recount her confession to the LAPD then testify for the prosecution would ensure her immunity.

The third break occurred when Lamar Duane Cady, 25, aka Fang, a Coyote acolyte and marginally mentally-deficient biker gang member of the Skull Helmets, rambled about both the Self and the Gallo murders while drunk and belligerent in the presence of rival bikers belonging to the Straight Satans.

A Satan secretly recorded Cady's ramblings, then exchanged the tape for a substantial amount of crystallized methamphetamine with an "operative" who in turn sold the tape to the LAPD for a "six figure fee," according to insiders.

On the strength of these confessions the task force moved to apprehend Coyote and pertinent tribe members. Ten days later, four of Coyote's tribe were in detention, but not the demonically charismatic leader himself.

Meanwhile, the Los Angeles District Attorney Office assigned Deputy DA Leo Dickerson to prosecute the coveted, high-profile case, assisted by Deputy DA Howard Feldman. Dickerson, 42, *magna cum laude* from UCLA, ex-president of the California Young Republicans, and graduate of Yale University Law School, was considered the brightest, most rigorous, and—in the view of his detractors—most ruthlessly ambitious prosecutor in the LADA office.

Leveling the Karma of the Rich

Transcripts

20 Dec '69

Deputy DA Leo Dickerson to LA County DA Office

Post

CC: LAPD, LASO

Listed below are the 4 Coyote tribe members in custody and 12 others still at large in connection with one or more of the following homicides: Self party; Gallo party; musician Andy Hassler; ranch-hand Bobby Steele; Black Panther "Lotsapoppa."

Since his release from Terminal Island Federal Prison in Jan '67 after serving 12 years for transporting stolen property over state lines and "white slavery," Coyote could be implicated in as many as 29 murders.

We estimate that up to 400 adolescents and teenagers lived and traveled with Coyote between May '67 and the brutal mass murders on 8 and 9 Aug '69. From San Francisco Coyote and his followers traveled to the Redwood forests north of Mendocino as far as Washington state. They then reversed direction and moved south through Nevada, Utah, back into California, settling in the LA area, where they camped in localities both near the city and in Death Valley. They traveled in Coyote's Black "Scorpion" bus as well as in cars and campers, with hippie hitchhikers appearing and disappearing at frequent intervals.

Aside from those in custody (asterisked), there are approximately 45-55 current Coyote followers squatting in the Harker Movie Ranch in the Simi Hills; in the Funeral Mountains area of Death Valley; or elsewhere in the greater LA vicinity.

Jesus Coyote, 35, aka Soul, Satan, the Great Chingon. Mastermind of the murders on Joya Grove and Bel Air.

Kyle Sean Embry, 24, aka Tex. Suspected of being Coyote's designated hit-man in the Self and Gallo murders.

Bruce Keith, 32, aka Sarge. Ex-con, suspect in the Bobby Steele murder.

***Billy Sans-Soleil**, 22, aka Cupid. Ex-porn actor. Convicted for the Andy Hassler murder.

Joe Don O'Malley, 28, aka Donkey Don. Suspect in the Gallo and Lotsapoppa murders.

Lamar Duane Cady, 25, aka Fang. Skull Helmet biker. Suspect in the Steele murder.

***Roxanne Bakramp**, 21, aka Roxi. Ex-porn actress and prostitute. Convicted for the Hassler murder and a primary suspect in the Self and Gallo murders.

***Bette Mulder**, 20, aka Bitch. Suspect in the Self and Gallo murders.

***Patricia Cheech**, 21, aka Chong. Ex-Marin County real estate trainee. Suspect in the Self and Lotsapoppa murders.

Hedda Hayman, 20, aka Head Games. Ex-lingerie model and wilderness advocate. Coyote spokesperson.

LuAnn Hoy, 20, aka Ho. Ex-standup comedienne from Nutley, New Jersey. Suspect in the Self murders.

Gloria Guillen, 18, aka Glori Hole. Ex-street prostitute from El Paso. Suspect in the Steele murder.

Elizabeth Ginzburg, 17, aka Li'l Bess. Suspected of involvement in the Self murders. Requesting immunity in exchange for testimony.

Lori-Kay Woerman, 15, aka Worm. Runaway from evangelical Christian home in Broken Arrow, Oklahoma. Suspect in the Self and Gallo murders.

Grace Jan Kaiserling, 18, aka GJ. Suspect in the Self murders.

Marie Weston, 29, aka Mercy. Ex-University of California librarian. Oldest female among the current tribe.

20 Dec '69
Jaroslav Hora to Deputy DA Leo Dickerson
Post

Apologies for not replying sooner. It is not every day a film director loses his beautiful eight-months pregnant wife through a senseless, bloody murder. It's flung me into a deep depression which has made it hard to communicate; but obviously I want to see that the swine responsible for the atrocities are fully prosecuted. I fly from Cannes where my current film is up for an award to LA on Sunday, so barring the unforeseen, my attorney and I will be in your office at the appointed time on Monday.

You realize, of course, that I was summoned to LA immediately after the massacre, was interrogated by the LAPD at some length, and even administered a lie detector test. I know that you weren't at that point the prosecutor of the case; still I would ask you to review the transcript of my LAPD interview to avoid needless repetition.

In response to some of your preliminary questions: I am a Czech Jew on my father's side and a Polish non-Jew on my mother's side. I was born in Brno, (birthplace of Freud), moved to Krakow when I was 6, then to Paris when I was 10. My father was a well-known architect who received important commissions in and out of France. My mother was a poet who also wrote cookbooks. Her language of choice was French.

I met Naomi Self six years ago when she acted in a film of mine, which—for reasons I won't get into—I later disowned. The subject was vampires, and Naomi was gorgeous with a fresh and affecting way of presenting herself on screen. But the fact is I wasn't especially interested in her until after the film was a wrap. We spent a weekend together at my cottage in Malibu. We walked along the shore, danced, made love, and I realized that I had never before met a girl that was so tender, so generous-spirited.

Naomi knew about my so-called womanizing but didn't care; she simply wanted us to want each other when we were together. We fell in love, she left Don Fernando, with whom she was living, and we moved in together—when, that is, we both happened to be in the US at the same time.

The murdered child in her belly was a male; we were planning to name him Che, not Cher, as has been falsely reported.

That is as much as I am prepared to say here.

20 Dec '69
Ho to Worm
Phone

You catch Li'l Dick's attack on Soul? It was all over the tube, Dickerson going on about Coyote's low IQ & how dumb his tribe fems must be to worship this "yy dummy."

When & where did they test Soul's intelligence? Probably in one of the jails they threw him in, or the damn reform school. Now how's a dirt-poor kid from Appalachia been in jail most his life gonna know what the Parthenon is? Ask him what a rat is. Ask him how a 10-year-old kid, not even five feet tall, gonna fight off a dozen slobbering cons with their cocks all out.

Soul knows more in the rim of his asshole than this attorney fool knows with his shitty law degree. He's the deputy DA in the LA office that's supposed to prosecute the tribe & he wants to make top dog real fast. Know what? Mr. Lawyer Dickerson's still gonna have a l'il dick even when he makes DA & Governor, or whatever. If he lives that long.

Worm, don't forget we're meeting outside the LA County Jail at 9 a.m.

Monday for the vigil—show our love & support for Soul & the tribe that's inside: Roxi, Bitch, Cupid, Chong. Jail's at Temple & Broadway, top two floors of the so-called Hall of Justice.

Call Head Games, Mercy, Mooch, GJ & Glori to remind them about the posters.

Contact Fang too. Him & his Skull Helmet kick-ass bros should be there Monday to support & protect Soul's sluts.

Don't call L'il Bess. Word is she's planning to cop a plea, testify against Soul & the tribe. Pissy little ingrate.

20 Dec '69
Deputy DA Leo Dickerson to LA County DA Office
Post
CC: LAPD, LASO

My office just learned that Colonel Kenyon Self, the murdered actress's father, has resigned from the Special Forces effective immediately, and has signaled to some of his associates that he's "going after" Coyote. To that end, Col Self has grown a full beard and Rasta-type braids and is preparing to drive out to the Raven Gulch Homestead in the Funeral Mountains area of Death Valley where Coyote and most of his tribe have been squatting. Our sources say that Col Self, a weapons expert, has armed himself with a Beretta nine mm, Winchester 12-gauge, and Mauser machine pistol.

We can only respect and admire a father's love for his beautiful pregnant, daughter and potential grandson, and we duly honor his rage at her brutal murder. But in a democracy even despicable hoodlums like Coyote and his tribe must be innocent until proven guilty in a court of law. That is their inalienable right.

Vigilantism is not the way to proceed. At the very least it will complicate an already complicated case, and if the Colonel actually shoots up a bunch of these scumbags it might just kill the case altogether.

I will convey to Col Self our concerns. Additionally, I am asking one desk officer from the LAPD and another from LASO to contact the Colonel by phone ASAP. His contact information is on file in both offices.

21 Dec '69
Worm to Ho
Phone

chong got to me through a fem was in the holding tank with her. Soul had contacted chong, bitch & roxi & said to do a tat on themselves, swastika between the eyes. it's a nazi deal—Soul wants the world to see the tribe's being treated like nazis by the real damn nazis, li'l dick & his fools.

mooch & glori said that if the jailed sluts do the swastika between the eyes tat, we should too, testimony of our undying love for him. I think it'd look cool at the vigil.

yeah, I heard l'il bess is coppin'. she's carrying Soul's seed in her damn belly. What else she fuckin' want?

21 Dec '69
Deputy DA Leo Dickerson to LA County DA Office
Post
CC: LAPD, LASO

As you well know, nine horrific murders were committed within two days. We have rounded up key suspects, though not the ringleader, Jesus Coyote. Even when we do apprehend him we could have a problem getting him executed or even putting him away for life, since there is a fair chance, according to the available intelligence, that Coyote may have instigated and blueprinted those and other murders without himself physically committing them.

However, something else has just come up, which if borne out, would help our case. One of the Coyote tribe on our suspects list, in exchange for a promise to *consider* immunity, came to our office for questioning about two other murders he claims Coyote committed himself, physically. The first alleged murder is of the African-American dope dealer and ex-Black Panther known as "Lotsapoppa," t/n Booker Malik Johnson. The second is of Bobby Steele, a bit-part movie actor and former employee on the Harker Movie ranch in the Santa Susana Mountains, where the Coyote tribe lived before transferring to Death Valley.

The Coyote tribe member seeking immunity is Joe Don O'Malley, 28, called "Donkey Don" by the cult girls because of his over-developed genitals.

My co-prosecutor Howard Feldman and I interrogated O'Malley in my office last night (20 Dec). O'Malley is a lanky, tattooed individual, with stringy, shoulder-length, blond hair, a walrus mustache and clouded-over gray eyes. He kept sniffling, as if he had a mean cocaine habit. Transcript follows.

Mr. O'Malley, tell us who Lotsapoppa was and what happened between him and Jesus Coyote.

Lotsapoppa dealt drugs. Sumo-size spade claimed he was a Black Panther with Huey Newton in Oakland. He said he gave a sack of blow and meth to Tex—

Explain who Tex is and when this event transpired.

Tex Embry from the tribe, Soul's right-hand man, 'cept he was always fuckin' up and always stoned. He been with Soul since the Haight which is where Soul crashed when he got out the joint the last time. Folsom, I think it was. What I'm talking about happened right before last Christmas, I can't tell you the exact date, maybe a week before Christmas, in, what?, '68. Anyways, Lotsapoppa's story was he sold blow and meth to Tex, $1500 worth. Tex didn't have the cash, so he left a hundred and Chong, one of the fems, as collateral, saying he'd be back that same night with the jack. Only he never went back.

Where was he?

Cain't say. He didn't come back to the ranch. Knowin' Tex, he was shackin' up with some fem or two and snortin' meth. The next a.m., Lotsapoppa calls the ranch, gets on the phone with Soul, says if he ain't paid by noon he gonna fuck Chong's brains out, then slice her up. Then go to the ranch, cut up whoever he finds there.

You witnessed this conversation?

Yeah, bunch of us was drinking coffee in the old saloon where the phone was at. Lotsapoppa was talkin' real loud and Soul was like grinning, holding the phone away from his head so we all could hear. Soul tells Lotsapoppa no prob, he'll be right over take care of the situation. He hangs up and tells me to go with him. Soul takes the old Buntline .22, sticks it in his belt. Big mother with a 10-inch barrel.

Where was the gun before he took it?

His room in one of the outbuildings. Soul was the only one had his own space. Rest of us slept in a dorm setup or where we could. So me and Soul get in the old Edsel and drive out to Watts, spadesville, where Lotsapoppa's crashin'—

Who drove?

Soul. So we go in the building and Lotsapoppa opens the door real mad and stoned on something, probly THC. We see Chong spread-eagled on the bed, naked, her body bruised and shit. Plus the place smells real funky, like Lotsapoppa been doin' some primo fuckin'.

The spade is holding out his big black mitt for the cash and Soul, real calm-like, tells him he don't have no cash for him. So then Lotsapoppa grabs him hard around the waist and lifts him up. Next thing I hear is a click, like the old Buntline misfired. Which makes Lotsapoppa grin real wide.

He says to Soul, "I'ma gon' back to your place and pin your eyes open with toothpicks, make you watch while them hoes yours suck my big black dick. Then I'ma cut them up. Sheat, while I'm at it, mebbe I'll eat a few of 'um." Lotsapoppa laughs real loud. Meantime he's squeezin' Soul like to kill him when I hear a second click, then a muffled shot, and I watch the black Sumo slide down dead like a humongous sack of shit.

Yeah, the old Buntline finally fired and Soul nailed him a 350 pound Black Panther nig with a single .22 round. I guess them Panthers ain't so tough like they make out.

Did the girl—Chong—also witness the murder?

Nah. She was out of it. Glazed-like. Probly from all the fucking Lotsapoppa was layin' on her.

You were the only witness?

Yup.

What happened next?

Soul told me cut Chong loose, which I done.

You carried a knife?

Swiss Army pocket knife.

What then?

We drove back to the Ranch. Stopped off at a diner for coffee and pie.

What kind of pie?

What kind? Peach, I think. Soul had berry. Cain't remember what Chong ate. Maybe berry. Same like Soul.

There are people at the diner that would testify to seeing you three together?

Hell, was a while ago. Lotsa folks chowin' down.

That was it? No repercussions? Nothing more from Lotapoppa's side? The Black Panthers?

Far as I know.

What happened to the gun, the old Buntline .22 with the ten-inch barrel?

Cain't say. Never seen it again.

Did Coyote mention the murder to anyone or refer to it in any way?

Not as such. Soul's deal was different. He'd say shit without really saying it straight. Use his eyes and shit. Signal with his hands like.

Why didn't he communicate the normal way?

Cain't say. Guess he thought that was the way Gods—or devils—s'pose to do it.

Did you think Coyote was a God or a devil?

Entered my mind.

Did Coyote's devil talk scare you?

Let's say it made me precautious.

Why didn't you leave?

Where I spose to go?

What about the murder of the ranch hand, Bobby Steele? Were you involved in that one?

No way. I ain't got the stones to put out no one's lights.

But you witnessed the murder?

Not as such. I heard about it. Soul was real slick with a knife and machete. With any kind of blade, really. Him and a bunch the tribe got a hold of Bobby, Soul put the chop to the cowboy, cut him real bad, then everyone stabbed at him, then they cut his head off, sliced up his body, buried it in like a bunch of places on the ranch. That's what I heard.

What did Coyote have against Bobby Steele?

Well, Bobby wasn't real happy 'bout the maroons crashing—

Are the maroons another name for the tribe?

Far as I know.

Does the name—maroon—have any particular significance?

Cain't really say.

Continue with what you were saying about Bobby Steele and Coyote.

Bobby wasn't happy 'bout the bunch of us crashing at the movie ranch and talked with old Jess about it. Jess Harker. Soul didn't like that. Me, I thought Bobby Steele was pretty cool. He never bothered me or nothin'. Thing is, Soul could get the tribe to do what he wanted even they wasn't sure why they doin' it.

How did Coyote manage this? Was it some kind of mass hypnotism?

Cain't really say.

Why are you testifying against Coyote? We know you're seeking immunity but is there any other reason?

When I joined up with the tribe Soul told me "go fuck my sluts." I done just that, okay, and got me a horrible case of the clap.

Just clap? Not syphilis, herpes, chlamydia?

The doc said was the Bangkok clap.

You don't still have it, do you?

Naw. But it took me a whole damn year to get rid of it.

What happens when Coyote hears that you've fingered him?

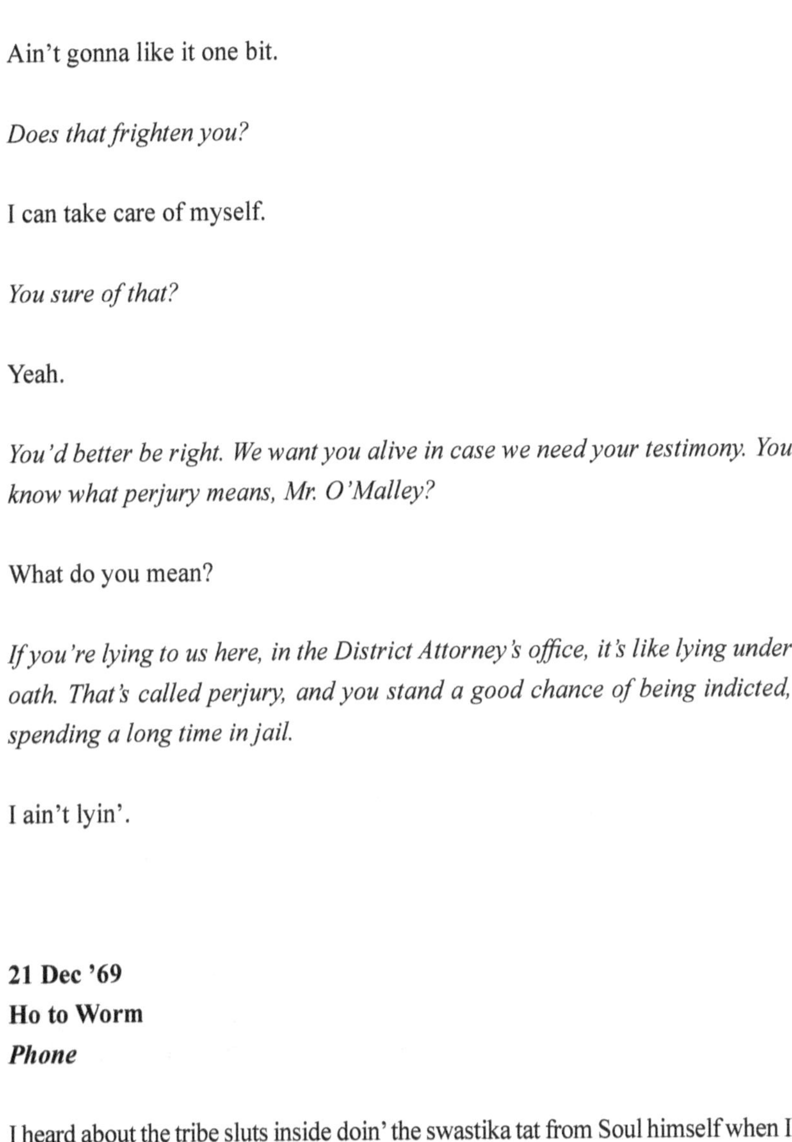

Ain't gonna like it one bit.

Does that frighten you?

I can take care of myself.

You sure of that?

Yeah.

You'd better be right. We want you alive in case we need your testimony. You know what perjury means, Mr. O'Malley?

What do you mean?

If you're lying to us here, in the District Attorney's office, it's like lying under oath. That's called perjury, and you stand a good chance of being indicted, spending a long time in jail.

I ain't lyin'.

21 Dec '69
Ho to Worm
Phone

I heard about the tribe sluts inside doin' the swastika tat from Soul himself when I was trippin'. Soul conveyed that Chong stole a spoon from the mess & sharpened it, then one of the other inmates cut the tat on her. Soul said if we cut a tat into our skin we'll be all swollen & it probably won't show clear by Monday.

What Soul said is we all shave our heads & paint the tat between our eyes so it shows sharp & clear. Soul said wear all black minis with no panties underneath, give the fools a thrill. We'll be like sexy swastika tribe-nuns: you, me, Mooch, Glori, Mercy, GJ, Loca, Head Games. Soul's sluts with their heads all shaved & a big ol' swastika between the eyes plus nothin' a'tall coverin' our poon.

Let's do the skinhead-tats thing tonight at GJ's step-mom's place, in Venice. Can't wait to see our pix on TV, huh?

21 Dec '69
Jaroslav Hora to Marie-Charlotte Blanchot
Post

What you read in *Le Monde* about the murderous cult ringleader is almost wholly untrue. *Le Monde* should have conferred with me before writing their typical leftish *merde.*

What I've learned from reliable sources is the following: Coyote was not born in the deep south, as *Le Monde* has it, but in West Virginia. His mother was a thief and street-hooker who spent most of her life in prison, not the poor abandoned widow in *Le Monde*'s version. Coyote himself is not 33-years-old, as *Le Monde* says, but 36. Coyote uses 33 to enforce his opportunistic identification with Jesus. Nor is Coyote "half a head taller than the diminutive film director," as *Le Monde* puts it. Coyote is listed as five-feet-four, which is an inch-and-a-half shorter than I am.

I especially resent *Le Monde's* version of the murder scene. There was **no** orgying going on among the five victims. Don Fernando's obligation was to look after my eight-months-pregnant wife, which is what he was doing. Don Fernando long ago made his peace with Naomi leaving him to live with me. The Joya Grove house is very large, and Viktor and Kristin were in a different wing.

The fifth victim was a teenager in his car who was visiting the caretaker.

My wife was brutally murdered but not sexually mutilated, as in *Le Monde's* version. I had the autopsy report sent to me and could have enlightened *Le Monde* had they consulted me. It is all so maddeningly banal.

Tomorrow I fly to the US—not with any enthusiasm, I assure you—to testify.

Planning to return to France as soon as possible, most likely in a week or so. I will let you know.

22 Dec '69
Deputy DA Leo Dickerson to LA County DA Office
Post
CC: LAPD, LASO

After receiving word that Coyote's tribe-girls were preparing some kind of demonstration in support of their guru outside the Hall of Justice, co-prosecutor Howard Feldman and I interrogated two of Coyote's head girls last night (Sat, 21 Dec) in my office.

They are LuAnn Hoy and Hedda Hayman, both 20-year-olds. Hoy is a slender, small-featured blonde and Hayman is a slender redhead with the robotic bright-eyed stare of a cult follower. Both are runaways, Hoy from Nutley, New Jersey, Hayman from Escondido, CA. Hayman is thought to be Coyote's most trusted acolyte.

There was no defense counsel present at the interview of the two girls. And we expect to hear from defense attorney Blumenthal on that score.

Hedda, tell us about the demonstration Coyote's girls have planned for Monday morning. Remember, if you lie to us you will be perjuring yourself and risking imprisonment.

Hedda: There's no law against demonstrating that I know of.

LuAnn: I never heard of one.

There is no law against demonstrating so long as the demonstration is not violent or obstructive. What did you have in mind?

(no response)

Let's have it, LuAnn. What are you girls planning to do on behalf of your guru?

Hedda: He's not a guru. He's a God.

LuAnn: You two worship money & power, but you still must know what a God is.

Coyote is the second coming of Jesus, right?

Hedda: It's not a joke. Money-mad sinners like you will be crucified on a cross of gold.

LuAnn: Soul performed miracles.

Hedda: Soul could turn even you two into feeling humans. Only you'd have to be receptive & submit.

LuAnn: They're too uptight to submit.

Tell us about the miracles.

LuAnn: He breathed life into a dead rattler. I saw it myself. The rattler rattled its tail & slithered away. He breathed life into a dead bird, too. A black & gold oriole. It flew away chirping.

Hedda: When GJ had her baby, Persephone, Soul cut the cord with his teeth.

LuAnn: He sewed it up with a guitar string.

Hedda: Then he went out & got fresh, cool water, even though there was no water any place near.

LuAnn: Some of us—we saw him stop a mountain lion in its tracks just by looking at it.

Hedda: Coyotes loved him. Soul would yip like a coyote & they would come out of the desert & lick his hands.

LuAnn: Here's one they will like. A new girl who just swallowed 300 migs of Orange Sunshine—

LSD?

LuAnn: Yes, daddy. LSD. The new girl was going down on Soul & she bit his cock off, had the crown of Soul's beautiful cock in her mouth. You know what Soul did? He ran his hand gentle over her face & just like that his great big hard-on was back together.

Hedda: It's true. I saw it. Bunch of us were watching—

We get the picture. Coyote is the God of fuck. Isn't that what he called himself?

Hedda: You make it sound dirty. We're not old & decrepit like you. Fuck for us is love.

LuAnn: Love is fuck too.

Love between male and female?

LuAnn: Between whatever.

Hedda: Male / female, female / male—You're too hung up on categories.

When did Jesus Christ become the God of fuck?

LuAnn: Jesus Christ wasn't the uptight guilt manager you all think he was. The real Jesus was sexy. He roamed the desert with longhaired boys & girls, apostles. He despised corrupt authority. He chased the money-changers from the temple. He preached love.

Hedda: Jesus Christ was love & sex until the church fathers captured his body & made up lies about him.

LuAnn: Like what these lawyers want to do with Soul.

Hedda: They'll never, ever do it.

Did Soul always demonstrate the kind of loving he advocated?

Hedda: Everything we did, Soul guided us.

LuAnn: Soul is our guide in everything.

So he—Soul—would have himself bound naked to a makeshift cross while his tribe orgied beneath him.

Hedda: Makeshift cross. That's one I never heard before.

LuAnn: Someone's been passing you tainted information, counselor.

You say that never happened. Okay. What about Soul going down on a young boy, or even an infant, to show that love had no barriers? Or sodomizing one of the new girls—fucking her in the ass? He would do this in front of the entire tribe, right? Everyone naked.

Hedda: Soul never did anything against anyone's will.

LuAnn: Why would he? There would be no point.

How much will does an infant have, girls?

Hedda: How much will does a shackled prisoner have? How much will does a leopard in a cage have?

LuAnn: How much will does a homeless person have? You know how many homeless there are in this country, counselor?

Hedda: How much will does a polluted birch tree have? More than you can imagine.

We're not talking about trees. We're talking about the so-called love-fests the tribe had. How frequent were they?

LuAnn: All the time. Wouldn't you like to get naked & make love all the time? Pull off your tie & shirt & suspenders. I know that lawyers always wear suspenders.

Hedda: These lawyers have fat tummies. I think they've forgotten what it feels like to get naked.

What kinds of drugs did you use at the love-fests? LSD, ecstasy, grass, coke?

Hedda: You people get too worked up about drugs. Look at you two with your suits & ties & suspenders. You're flabby, your eyes are bloodshot. You're addicted to work, money-making. You'd be better off swallowing a drug, going back home & making love with your wife. What do your wives do while you're here calculating how to make money?

LuAnn: Their wives are lawyers like them.

The Coyote tribe-girls we've seen are all very thin. Is that because you are vegetarians?

LuAnn: What would you like us to eat?

Hedda: Cheeseburgers, so we can become fat little good girls who marry lawyers & worship money like they do.

You get your food from restaurant and supermarket garbage bins, isn't that right?

Hedda: It's perfectly good food that markets & restaurants throw away simply because it is bruised or discolored.

LuAnn: Another example of foolish capitalist waste. There are starving, homeless people out there.

Hedda: They never noticed. The only humans they notice are the ones they can rip off.

Enough of the insults, girls. Is this demonstration tomorrow going to be a love-fest for the God of Fuck?

Hedda: Yes, daddy.

LuAnn: Everything we do for Soul is a love-fest.

Coyote is so tiny. It would be like watching a dwarf copulate. How sexy is that, LuAnn?

Hedda: We don't know about copulate, but let me tell you two flabby lawyers something: Soul fucking is beyond your capacity to imagine.

LuAnn: You two males are old & flabby. But you still got to fuck, right? Every insect's got to fuck.

You'd be advised to keep an eye on your insect god. We're talking about Jesus Coyote, mass murderer. He's looking to sting you all in the ass to save his own ass. You can go now.

23 Dec '69
Defense attorney R. Jack Blumenthal to Deputy DA Dickerson
Post

As the "Tribe's" head counsel, I am compelled to register my gravest concerns re the tactics that you and your co-prosecutor Mr. Feldman employed in interrogating two 20-year-old girls, LuAnn Hoy and Hedda Hayman, in your office on Saturday night, 21 Dec, without counsel present.

Our understanding is that you posed leading questions to Misses Hoy and Hayman with the intention of entrapping them into betraying the whereabouts of Jesus Coyote.

We have reported your action to the Office of the Bar of the state of California. We maintain that your cynically unethical "interview" constitutes valid warrant to dismiss you from the trial, and/or to declare a mistrial. We are hopeful that the LADA will concur.

23 Dec '69
Ho to Worm, Mooch, Hedda, Glori, Mercy, GJ
Real time

We done it, Soul sluts. Shaved & swastika'd & all in black with no drawers. We stopped traffic, didn't we? I can see Soul's face. He woulda dug the shit out of it.

Soul conveyed to me when I was trippin'—He said keep supporting him in these creative ways & we'll spring Cupid & the tribe sluts & there's no kinda way the Man's gonna keep Soul down.

Did you catch the looks on the faces of the fools in their cars & walkin' by? But the best deal is TV, they were fuckin' all over it, & channel 10 news like even went on about the no panties with shots of GJ, Worm & me showin' sweets. Way cool.

23 Dec '69
Deputy DA Leo Dickerson to LA County DA Office
Post
CC: LAPD, LASO

Our office has learned that Colonel Kenyon Self attempted suicide on the night of 21 Dec by shooting himself in the chest with a Smith & Wesson .38 Police Special. Remarkably, the single .38 round passed through his chest and out his back without affecting vital organs. Colonel Self is now in a Marin County-area hospital in serious condition. His wife, Laraine Day Self, traveled from Boulder, Colorado, where she was visiting family, to be at her husband's bedside. Their 22-year-old daughter Nara, the murdered actress's "kid sister," and an actress herself, is also by her father's side. Fortunately, Colonel Self is expected to make a full recovery. Our prayers go out to the Colonel and his bereaving family.

24 Dec '69
Deputy DA Leo Dickerson to LA County DA Office
Post
CC: LAPD, LASO

Before getting to the interview with Jaroslav Hora, we should comment on the spectacle outside the Hall of Justice on Temple and Broadway by Coyote's female acolytes. They shaved their heads, painted swastikas between their eyes and pranced around in short black skirts without underwear, while surrounded by Skull Helmet bikers.

Moronically adolescent as the display was, some media found it "uncanny," and "demonic," which could have an inhibiting effect on the testimonies once the trial begins. Nonetheless, we remain wholly confident that the weight of the evidence against this madman and his cult will triumph.

The murdered actress's husband, movie director Jaroslav Hora, arrived at my office on Monday a.m., accompanied by his attorney Dale Robertson. Co-prosecutor Feldman and I interviewed him as follows:

This office as well as the LAPD have contacted you before while you were in Europe, so you will excuse us if there's some repetition in the questions. Can you think of any reason that your wife and her companions inside 5 Hoya Drive would be targeted for murder?

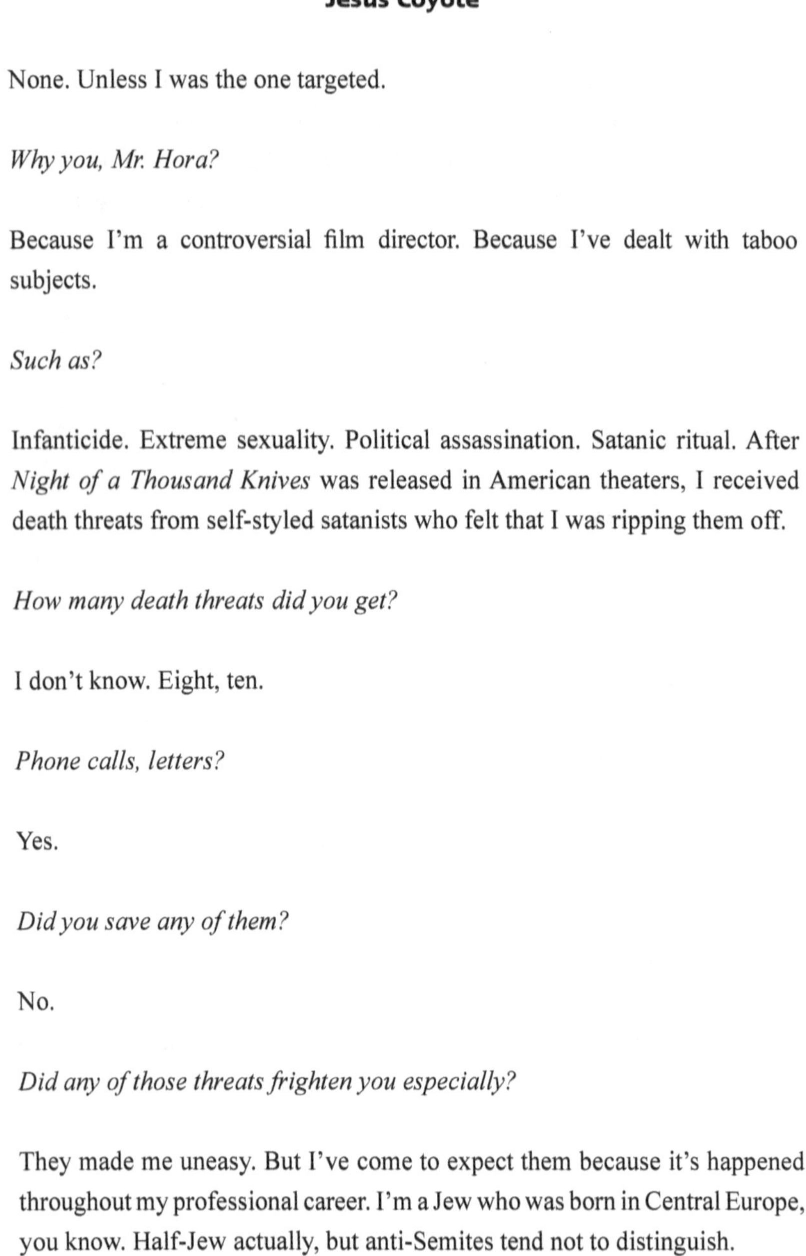

None. Unless I was the one targeted.

Why you, Mr. Hora?

Because I'm a controversial film director. Because I've dealt with taboo subjects.

Such as?

Infanticide. Extreme sexuality. Political assassination. Satanic ritual. After *Night of a Thousand Knives* was released in American theaters, I received death threats from self-styled satanists who felt that I was ripping them off.

How many death threats did you get?

I don't know. Eight, ten.

Phone calls, letters?

Yes.

Did you save any of them?

No.

Did any of those threats frighten you especially?

They made me uneasy. But I've come to expect them because it's happened throughout my professional career. I'm a Jew who was born in Central Europe, you know. Half-Jew actually, but anti-Semites tend not to distinguish.

You ***don't*** *have copies of any of those threats you received?*

I never thought to save them.

None in particular stand out as seeming especially dangerous or menacing?

Hard to say. I've thought about this since Naomi's murder. No, I haven't really been able to single out any one of them.

Have you ever come in contact with Jesus Coyote?

Never.

What about his followers? Members of his so-called tribe? Have you ever come in contact with any of them?

I wouldn't know, since I don't know who they are. I saw the girls with shaved heads and swastikas on TV. Completely loony. I'd never seen any of them before.

You of course knew all four people in the Joya Grove house that night: Your wife, hairstylist Don Fernando, Viktor Hus and Kristin Barrett.

Yes.

Then you must have known that both Hus and Don Fernando were drug users and drug dealers. Especially Hus—

(Hora's lawyer interrupts to advise his client not to respond to the "leading question.")

Okay. I'll put it this way. Mr. Hora, is there any reason that one or more of the people in the house that night would be targeted by murderers?

No.

Your deceased wife, Naomi Self, was a beautiful young woman. Did she ever indicate to you that she was being bothered or stalked or in any way troubled by a person or people?

Naomi was beautiful of course. She's been called one of the most beautiful women in the world. But she was also extraordinarily innocent and trusting. Even if she were being "stalked" she would not notice it.

Then it is possible, at least theoretically, that she was being stalked but did not mention it because it made no impression on her.

(Again Hora's lawyer advises his client not to answer.)

Mr. Hora, your late wife acted in your movie ***Vampire Daughters in Beverly Hills****, correct?*

Yes.

Did she have any interest in so-to-speak demonic matters? Satanism, devil-worship, that sort of thing?

Not at all. Did you see *Vampire Daughters in Beverly Hills?*

No, I'm afraid I didn't.

It's a comedy. Cut to shreds by my American producers. But it is still a comedy. Vampires are big business and there are probably twenty vampire movies a year. However, people who act in them aren't usually themselves vampires.

I realize that, Mr. Hora. Even if a question seems ill-informed, it is necessary to cover all the pertinent bases. I hope you can appreciate that.

Let's please continue.

When Naomi Self was in Amsterdam last summer she was observed visiting occult book shops in the Red Light District.

And what might that signify?

That's what we were hoping you would tell us.

Have you been to Amsterdam?

Briefly, yes.

Then you may have noticed that there are lots of things to do and look at in Amsterdam, including occult books. That my wife went into occult bookstores signifies nothing beyond an intelligent person exercising her curiosity.

Understood. On the other hand, you and your wife gave a number of parties at the Joya Grove residence. Occasionally with more than a hundred people in attendance, including partygoers unconnected with the film industry, such as bikers, street people and other hard core types, a lot of them crashers. Can you be certain that none of Coyote's tribe or even Coyote himself ever attended those parties?

Coyote's is a face I wouldn't forget. He was never in the Joya Grove house. About his cult followers, I can't say absolutely, but I wouldn't think any of them were in the Joya Grove house either.

Isn't it true that sado-masochistic sexual practices and occult sorts of happenings—satanism and so on—took place at those parties?

(Hora's lawyer objects to the "prejudicial" question.)

All right. Let me ask you this, Mr. Hora. You know that after the murder a considerable quantity of illegal substances were found in the house: LSD,

MDMA, cocaine, marijuana, hashish, methamphetamine.

Well?

What was the relationship among the victims?

What do you mean?

Were they all friends? Lovers? Who was lovers with whom?

(Hora's lawyer advises his client not to answer, but Hora responds.)

Viktor Hus and Kristin Barrett were lovers and living together. Obviously you and your task force know that. Don Fernando had been my wife's former lover, but that was long over. She was eight months pregnant and he was looking after her.

You know that your wife, lying in bed, was wearing bikini panties and a lacy top without a brassiere? And that Don Fernando, wearing just bikini briefs, was sitting on her bed?

I suppose you think it's necessary, but I find your question insinuating and in bad taste.

We apologize for our bad taste. There is a great deal at stake here and we are obliged sometimes to ask unpleasant questions.

Since everyone in Joya Grove was murdered, how would you know the physical configuration of the victims?

We have our methods.

There was neither an orgy nor a drug-fest going on in Joya Grove. If drugs were a factor, why didn't the murderers snatch all the drugs you say were present?

That's what we're trying to ascertain.

We're talking about Hollywood. Drugs are commonplace, you know that.

We know it all too well. We also know that a majority of the felonies committed in Hollywood have to do with drugs. For your information, Mr. Hora, Don Fernando, "hairstlylist to the stars," was also dope-pusher to the stars. Of that we have unimpeachable evidence. And Viktor Hus was evidently the prime conduit of MDMA from Israel and the Netherlands to the western US.

I find that hard to believe. I couldn't imagine Viktor bothering himself with all that responsibility. We were old friends and I know that he had a substantial independent income. He was engaged to Kristin who was the Phillip Morris heiress and worth millions. Why would he want to smuggle MDMA or anything else?

People do unpredictable things sometimes. What about Don Fernando?

Arguably *the* major hairstylist in Hollywood and quite wealthy.

To your knowledge, then, Don Fernando was not dealing drugs when he was living with Naomi Self?

No. Obviously I knew less about him than about Naomi. And I know that Naomi did not have much experience with drugs outside of cannabis. I read the coroner's report; no drugs were found in her system.

True. On the other hand, a considerable amount of drugs was found in the others. Hashish, cocaine and MDMA in Viktor Hus. Cocaine and hashish in Don Fernando. MDMA in Kristin Barrett.

So. Lawyers drink single malt scotch and martinis. Hollywood people prefer drugs.

(Hora's lawyer: I'm not sure where this line of questioning is leading.)

What are your current plans, Mr. Hora?

What do you mean?

Are you planning on remaining in the Los Angeles vicinity for a while?

A week. I return to Paris Tuesday next.

It is our understanding that you've engaged a so-called psychic with whom you plan to visit Joya Grove.

How would you know that?

It had to be cleared with the special task force, who in turn contacted our office. Can we ask you what you expect this psychic to provide that our investigation has not provided?

I don't have any precise expectations. She—the psychic—has a good reputation, and friends recommended I consult her. It is my wife, my unborn child and my close friend who were murdered, you know. I have the right to do what I can.

Mr. Hora, please leave us the address and phone number where you are staying. In case something comes up and we need to contact you.

Let me ask *you* something. How close are you to capturing this lunatic—and whichever of his cult or tribe are still out there?

How close? I'm not in position to give you any sort of time line. I am certain that we will apprehend him. And we must make sure that when we have him we'll be able to prosecute him to the full extent of the law

24 Dec '69
Tex Embry to Worm
Phone

I totally dug what you & the tribe sluts done at the Hall of Justice yesterday. Soul musta been yipping. I wish I coulda been there but I cain't let myself be snatched. It's 3 a.m. & I'm on a pay phone.

What I heard is jew gal Ginzburg slut gonna be coppin' a plea to the grand jury, tellin' everything she knows about the actress' murder 'n' shit. Somebody should off her before she gets a chance. Yeah, I know she's carrying & Soul could be the jizz that jizzed her but it still gonna be a half-weasel-jew infant, right? I don't want no more traitor jews in my life, half, third or quarter.

See, I told Soul from the start no jews, because they all scummy turncoats from the first one Judas. And if they rich like jew gal slut it makes it worse 'cuz you know sooner or later they gon' trade silver for total fuckin' immunity. If we don't get to her we should whack her rich old man, the plastic surgeon, or her mama with her fixed-up nose. Shit, Soul hisse'f said Hitler leveled the karma of the jews. Let's fuckin' keep it that way.

You know what: I don't feel no guilt. Us maroons whacked some Hollywoods. So bleepin' what. It was a rip. I'd do it again, only better. I'd use that 3-ply nylon rope Soul gave, draw and quarter that hairdresser & Self, watch the damn jew fetus pop out. Then we'd lynch the jew Polack, show him some good ole Amerikkkan justice.

So guess who's prosecuting the so-called case against the tribe? jew Dickerson from the DA office. Super-ambitious, photo-op, nose-job jew with an eye on bigtime politics. Tell me what kind of justice we gon' get out of that?

Tribe sluts, I ain't gon' tell you where I'm at. Where I'm at is where they ain't a-gonna git me alive. If this sounds like I'm stoned, that's 'cuz I yam.

27 Dec '69
Jaroslav Hora to Marie-Charlotte Blanchot
Post

I mentioned that I was thinking of engaging a "psychic" to visit the massacre scene on Joya Grove. This psychic, who calls herself Cassandra (why not?), was well-recommended by some actor and director friends out here. But of course in California every sort of wackiness has its corps of followers. The crux of the matter is that the psychic and I, with permission from the police, visited the property, and, yes, it was freaky. Cassandra asked me for some intimate photos of Naomi that she could use in her "divination," and she passed those photos over different parts of the house where the walls were still bloodied (so much blood!).

When we left, Cassandra said her provisional impression was that three men, "two Black Muslims and one Hispanic," were responsible for the savagery and that the motives were drugs and anarchy. She asked to keep the photos for a while longer.

A week later I found the same photos reproduced in one of the spectacle tabloids with a garish headline underneath. Cassandra the psychic had sold the photos for a hefty sum and of course without my permission. When I phoned her for an explanation, I couldn't reach her. She got $10,000 from me and no doubt a good deal more from the tabloid. Call it applied capitalism.

And I'm scarcely in position to sue her; I don't have the heart for it. Which is what she banked on, I'm sure. *Filthy, filthy*.

I am writing to you from a friend's house in Malibu where the American paparazzi haven't yet found me. I fly to Paris on Tuesday. With any luck you and I will be having a *Ricard* at *La Coupole* Wednesday at around six.

29 Dec '69
Deputy DA Leo Dickerson to LA County DA Office, LAPD, LASO, LA Media Service
Press Conference

We are pleased to announce that the LAPD, LASO, along with detectives from the LADA and agents from the FBI, ATF and DEA, apprehended Jesus Coyote together with 15-year-old Lori-Kay Woerman, aka Worm, this a.m. at 5:45. They were nude and evidently asleep in a sleeping bag alongside the crevasse in the Funeral Mountains area of Death Valley that Coyote called Devil's Hole. The peculiar thing is that the sleeping bag was surrounded by a pack of coyotes that growled at us but then fled.

We ordered Coyote and Woerman out of the bag and they surrendered peaceably. In fact they wanted to be arrested and transported nude presumably to make some kind of "statement" about police brutality. They had to be forcibly dressed.

Coyote is being held under 24/7 armed surveillance in the Los Angeles County Jail, which occupies the upper two floors of the Hall of Justice, where the LADA will try the case.

There are a few principals in the Coyote tribe that we have yet to apprehend, though we fully expect to have them in custody within a short time. The important news is that we have the kingpin, Jesus Coyote.

We wish to thank the entire special task force team: the LAPD, the LASO, the FBI, the DEA, the Bureau of Alcohol, Tobacco and Firearms, and the US Marshals Service for their invaluable cooperation. Now it is up to us in the LADA to ensure that Coyote and his "tribe" of psychopathic acolytes are prosecuted to the full extent of the law.

1 Jan '70
Unidentified to Deputy DA Leo Dickerson
Post

This is to inform you that if you don't release Jesus Coyote within 48 hours we will hijack a commercial American aircraft & execute the passengers one every half-hour, until you *do* release him. If you think this is a prank or an idle threat you are sorely mistaken.

It is you all with your money mania & power mania & deathly fear of your own bodies that have infected this world. Soul is guilty of nothing but trying to re-infect this fucked-over world with love.

We prefer to die rather than occupy this world without Soul. So it does not matter to us if we fail to hijack the aircraft successfully. There are more than enough of us to keep trying until we succeed.

Be advised: If you do not release Soul, we will make this threat public so that people & especially potential passengers will freak out, while we follow through on the skyjacking.

2 Jan '70
Deputy DA Leo Dickerson to LA County DA Office,
LAPD, LASO, LA Media Service
Press Conference

As anticipated, the LA Special Task Force, with the cooperation of the San Antonio Police Department, have captured one of Jesus Coyote's chief lieutenants, Kyle Sean Embry, aka Tex, at his parents' home in Hondo, Texas, thirty miles west of San Antonio. The apprehension took place at 4:43 a.m., on 2 Sept.

Embry, who is suspected of involvement in both the Self and Gallo murders, surrendered without conflict and is now in custody under 24-hour surveillance in the Los Angeles County Jail, in a separate cell from Jesus Coyote.

Again, we thank the various law enforcement agencies, both statewide and federal, for their invaluable cooperation.

3 Jan '70
LA County Public Defender's Office to LA County DA Office
Post
CC: LAPD, LASO

Regarding the capture of Tex Embry, purported to be a confederate of cult leader Jesus Coyote, the LA Public Defender's Office which will represent Mr. Embry, is compelled to report that the recent phone call (date: 24 Aug, at 2:56 a.m.) traced to a pay phone in East Los Angeles and purportedly made by Mr. Embry to one of Coyote's female tribe members, Lori-Kay Woerman, aka Worm, is counterfeit.

The phone call was filled with defamatory anti-Semitic remarks directed at another of Coyote's tribe, Elizabeth Ginzburg, as well as at State Prosecutor Leo Dickerson.

When the phone call was made, Tex Embry himself was in his parents' home in Hondo, Texas, and that can be proven.

At this juncture, we have no idea who counterfeited the defamatory phone call in Tex Embry's name, but in the service of justice, it is essential to make clear that the bigoted sender was not Mr. Embry.

5 Jan '70
Deputy DA Leo Dickerson to LA County DA Office,
LAPD, LASO, LA Media Service
Press Conference

The LA Special Task Force apprehended three of Jesus Coyote's so-called tribe-fems, 8:40 a.m., at the Delta Airlines check-in counter at LAX Airport. One of the females was attempting to smuggle a Taurus 9 mm semi-automatic aboard the aircraft and another was attempting to smuggle a seven-inch Buck knife and a concoction made from LSD, evidently as a kind of virulent agent designed to sicken or even murder passengers and crew. The females, all of whom were previously under suspicion and wanted for questioning, were identified as Grace Joan Kaiserling, 18, aka GJ; Gloria Guillen, 18, aka Glori Hole; and Marie Weston, 29, aka Mercy.

Preliminary questioning indicates that the three females, in accord with their threatening post of 1 Jan, intended to hijack the aircraft scheduled to fly to New York, and to murder passengers one-by-one until Jesus Coyote was freed from custody. The females were remanded to the Los Angeles County Jail for further interrogation. The LADA will keep you updated.

8 Jan '70
LA Times Editors to LA County DA Office
Phone

We at the *Times* ask you to confirm an incident at the LA County Jail before we publish it. It was reported that the three Coyote girls interned for attempted skyjacking were in the exercise yard Friday a.m. when they heard Jesus Coyote, in his secluded cell in another part of the building, yipping and howling like a coyote. This provoked them into raising their dresses and yipping and howling like a band of coyotes back to Coyote. Evidently this back and forth went on until the prison guards appeared, at which time all three of the girls squatted on the cement and urinated. The guards had to forcibly escort the girls, who kept shouting "Soul's sluts," inside.

We understand that in order to get the girls away from Coyote's influence they have since been transferred to the Sibyl Brand Institute.

We are prepared to run this report substantially as outlined above. If your office has anything to add or controvert, please do so. If we do not hear from you we will assume that the weird event in this extraordinarily weird case happened as described and we will display it prominently in the Sunday edition of the *Times*.

Tribe of Coyote

Roxi
(19 years after, California Institute for Women, Frontera)

There have been a lot of lies written about me.

Like I joked once to a cellmate at Sybil Brand that I had sex with this dude and just when he was about to cum he shot himself in the head and all that blood and brain mess spurting everywhere gave me a monster orgasm. I said it would be cool to do that with Jim Morrison—shoot him in his sexy head with my Smith .38 and we'd bleed and cum together.

But then Jim Morrison got himself fat and died.

Anyways, I never did any of that stuff, I was just running my mouth. But my cellmate reported it to the warden and next thing it was all over the media.

Another time at Frontera I was going on about the Self killings and said that after plunging the knife in Naomi a bunch of times I tasted the blood off the knife and said: "Freaky shit, I like it." That too made big headlines in the papers and stuff.

Okay. First of all, I didn't plunge the knife in the beautiful pregnant Naomi a bunch of times. It's on record that Tex Embry was the one that did her. By the time I stabbed her she was already dead. Second of all, I never tasted her blood or said "Freaky shit, I like it." It was something I totally made up.

I was wrong to brag about it, I know. Insecurity has been like a monkey on my back, and I have a way of blurting out things that are exaggerated or flat-out not true. I know I'm pretty and sexy—well, I used to be. I don't look all that hot now. Hey, even Naomi Self is gonna look like shit after nineteen years in the slam with no chance for parole.

So if I was pretty and sexy back then why was I so uptight? I can't tell you. Maybe it was the black hole of not having Jesus in my life. Anyways, it was this insecurity that Soul glommed on to. One of Soul's gifts was spotting your weakness and using it to his advantage.

It was May '67, I was 18 and had been on my own for the last three years. My mother was dead of cancer. My father was just trying to hold on to a job and was glad I was out of the apartment, one less mouth to feed.

I was crashing in this house in Haight-Ashbury when I heard a guitar playing upstairs, and then I heard a soft, very romantic vocal singing along with the guitar. I was drawn upstairs to this room with a big bay window and under the window sitting cross-legged on cushions was Soul strumming and singing with his eyes closed. He was clean-shaven at that time, with smallish regular features and thick, wavy black hair. He was wearing dark gray work pants and a black tee shirt, and both of his forearms were tattooed. I could tell he was a small man from the way he looked sitting. He was surrounded by young girls with their eyes closed, swaying their hips. It was dusk and the soft pastel light angled through the bay window.

Soft the dark of your lips,
Softer the light in your eyes,
Fragrant the shadow of your hips,
Whirling, whirling through the bleeding heart of sky.

I stood at the doorway listening to his light baritone voice sing those strange, sweet words when he suddenly opened his eyes and without blinking or moving his head, looked right into my eyes. His eyes were intensely black and clear, with almost no iris around the pupil. It was like a laser boring into my soul.

Even though I had smoked some bud earlier and was feeling receptive, what I picked up from Soul at that moment wasn't like any other feeling I ever had. He closed his eyes again and I joined the girls around him. I started to sway along with some of them, then I started to dance. I was a good dancer, I'd danced topless for a living in North Beach, and I guess I wanted to show off, impress him.

Like I said, I was super sexy then. I was barefoot. My dark brown hair was shiny and so long I could sit on it. I was wearing a tiny black leather mini and pink sleeveless cotton sweater with no bra. Nobody wore bras then. As I was dancing suggestively with my eyes partly closed, I could see him lay down his guitar, get up from the cushions, and barefoot walk toward me. I remember thinking to myself: he's a very small man, delicate even.

Meanwhile an LP had come on—the Stones, I think—and as I was dancing, picking up the tempo, he came up behind me and started to dance with me from the back. Every time I turned, he would turn so that I couldn't see him, which I thought to myself was a weird sort of dance routine, and it went on for a while. Then he put his hands on my hips and pushed up on me from behind and I could feel his erection through my skirt. While we were dancing that way he was manipulating my body, moving me in ways that were new to me. And all the time he was whispering, almost crooning, in my ear. *"Do it now... Do it now... Die ... Do it... "*

I felt more than understood what those words meant, which is the way it always was with Soul. Suddenly he whirled me hard around and we were dancing against each other, his hands around my waist, our hips thrust out, his hard cock through his pants grinding into me.

Another hotter Stones track came on, Soul separated our bodies and we picked up the beat even more. Soul was always very quick and nimble on his feet. When we were in the desert he would scramble and stalk around like a coyote. Dancing, he was a maniac. Somebody once said that he danced like fire. He was completely free, and at the same time sort of menacing in his gestures, you had no idea what he would do next. But I was keeping up with him.

Then something weird happened. He pulled me very close to him and it was like he pulled me through him, like my body disappeared in his body, or merged identities with him. I felt for a second like I would pass out, but I recovered and continued dancing crazily, out of control, at the same time seeming to know what I was doing because I was in his body, and all the time he was whispering to me: *"Do it. Die. Now. Now."*

Haight maroons—which was Soul's name for counter-culture people—were usually too hip to be impressed, but they had formed a circle around us, snapping their fingers. They were digging it. Then it was over. The music stopped and we were standing there sweating and panting. Soul was holding both of my wrists and we were looking in each other's eyes.

Though he was smiling at me, his black iris-less eyes were looking through me, I could feel them like a sort of tickling behind my own eyes, inside my head.

In his soft voice he said, "Who are you?"

"Roxi."

"Coyote," he said. "People here call me Soul."

I didn't say anything.

"You're Roxi the rocker," he said. "I love the way you dance. You know what?"

I shrugged my shoulders.

"I'm going to have you dance like that right on my face." He laughed. Then he let go my wrists. "Follow me, Roxi.

I followed him into another smaller room down the hall. It smelled of incense and weed. Blankets were spread out on the wooden floor. On one wall was a floor-length mirror. Soul moved me in front of the mirror and said, "Get naked for me, Roxi."

I said I'd been on my own for a long time and for almost a whole year I danced topless and sometimes bottomless in the strip clubs of North Beach. I also did some raunchy spread shots for a studio that doubled as a whorehouse. So I fucked johns, did orgies—the whole shot. Girls won't admit it, but they imagine all kinds of shit, like, for example, doing three dudes, one for each hole. Well, I lived it, okay? Not just once but a bunch of times.

What I'm saying is naked was natural to me. Yet when Soul told me to undress I felt something I hadn't felt in a long time: inhibition, resistance. I been through a lot, but I never liked following orders. I was used to being in control, or at least thinking I was in control.

At the same time I felt in the deepest part of me that this was different. That Soul, small and slight as he was, was unlike anyone I'd ever encountered. So after hesitating, I pulled off my sweater and slipped out of my tiny skirt and panties.

The lovemaking was incredible. Again, it was as if we were in each other's body. All the movements were free, our bodies touching in all kinds of ways. Orgasms were easy for me, and I was used to getting off multiple times. But with

Soul the orgasms were explosive and at the same time natural, like breathing.

When Soul finally penetrated it was from behind, in my ass. I was used to that too and liked it okay. This time, though, it didn't hurt. Soul was large and surprisingly thick for such a small man, but somehow he slid right in. And then he rode me like he did when he danced behind me, only he was way up inside me. I felt the pulsing of his thick cock like it was some kind of live animal. My asshole pulsed along with him like tiny drumbeats. When after a long time he came, I felt the hot, thick spurts one after another high in my ass.

I was the third fem in Soul's tribe, after Head Games and Mercy, Marie Weston. After me came LuAnn Hoy, who we called Ho, and Loca, who was Daria Luz Shriver. Soul made up all the nicknames. And he also gave some of the fems—the ones closest to him—colors. He called Head Games green because of her feelings for wilderness. He called Worm red because she was sex-crazed. Me he called black because of my moods and the devil-type games I played.

Like when I was stripping in North Beach, the "Church of Satan" guy, Anton LaVey, caught my act and asked if I would play a vampire in one of his midnight mass things. The pay was good and I was curious, so I did it. Naked with lots of mascara and blood-red lipstick, I had to rise up like Dracula's daughter from a casket. Actually I was a little uptight so I dropped acid—250 migs of Sunshine—before being locked in the casket. It was far fuckin' out, let me tell you. The mass was filmed and I played it for Soul after we met. He dug it a lot.

At that time in the Haight, there was only one other dude besides Soul in the tribe, Bruce Keith, a husky, bearded older guy, very good-looking, an ex-con we called Sarge. Him and Soul got along real well from the start even though they didn't talk that much.

Head Games was that way too. Her and Soul seemed to have a silent understanding. I didn't know how she did it but it made me jealous. I wanted to be Soul's number-one tribe fem, and Soul quickly recognized my hang-up. Every once in a while he would get me alone and say something like, "You always want to be Queen Bee, don't you?"

"What's wrong with that?"

"It keeps you from chilling. Letting yourself be where you're at."

Another time, when I was in a snit and being real negative, Soul pulled me aside and said that if I wasn't careful one day I would start screaming and not be able to stop.

It hurt when he said that, but it was true. I've always felt a little crazy. I can't say why. But one thing I do know—if it wasn't for Jesus Christ I'd be a suicide or locked up in a loony bin someplace.

Though Soul had only been in the Haight for a few months, all the maroons knew him and talked about him. Something about the way he moved and talked and mastered his fems and played his music. A lot of people called him Wizard.

By the time we left San Francisco, there were too many of us for a car, so Soul scammed an old school bus that we painted black and named Scorpion. Soul and sometimes Sarge drove. First we went north into Oregon and Washington, then east into Montana and Idaho. Soul picked up maroons hitchhiking wherever we stopped, most but not all of them fems. Just about all of them were pretty and sexy too and Soul made a point of fucking every one, dudes included, which ticked me off at first. But Soul wasn't gay. I don't even think he was bi. What he was was an everything man. Sometimes he would fuck the new girls in private, in one of the curtained areas of the bus. Or he would do it right in the open when we were all squatting in a field sharing some bud.

Now and then Soul would pull the Scorpion off the road, and we'd do X or acid or mescaline and fuck orgy style. I always made a point of having him do me in the orgies because I wasn't getting that much of him any more. I have to say, though, that I dug fucking some of the other guys too, especially Sarge.

Never once did I think about where we were going or what we'd do when we got there. I just wanted to be near Soul and do what he wanted me to do. But with the numbers of the tribe increasing so fast, I wasn't getting any special attention, and it bugged me.

Soul picked up Tex Embry when we turned around and were heading for LA. Tex was hitching outside Santa Barbara. He was barefoot, a tall, rangy dude with a blond handlebar mustache and long hair combed in a kind of pageboy. It was a strange look but it was also sexy.

After Tex came aboard the Scorpion Soul told Sarge to pull the bus over to the shoulder. He motioned Tex to sit on the cushions in the center of the bus where he usually sat. Then he filled up a basin with water and washed Tex's feet very gentle, not saying a word. Tex just laid back with a surprised expression on his face. After Soul finished, he motioned me to go with Tex behind the curtains, which we did. I fucked Tex then and many times after that. He was a real good cocksman.

I've had a long time in solitary to think about those early days in the Scorpion and later in LA and Death Valley. I don't know if there was a single day where I wasn't stoned on something and sexing with someone, or more than one. Yet I almost always felt on the out, needy. This great need I identified with Soul because he was by far the most charismatic presence and—we all thought—the largest spirit. What he actually was was Lucifer, or some form of the devil, masking as the true God. I learned later, with Jesus in me, that that's what devils do: they mask as Jesus to parasitize our bodies and our spirits. Once in control, they make us do things we never would have considered doing. This sounds like I'm copping out of the responsibility for the terrible crimes I committed. What I mean to say was I was weak with a deep black hole of need in me, and in my condition I was ripe pickings for the devil Coyote.

How could I know then that what I needed to fill the black hole was total submission to the true Jesus? How much torment would I have to go through to know it? How much torment would I have to inflict on others before I learned to love Him?

Once, at the movie ranch, at a time when things seemed to be going good and Soul was not all paranoid about the Man and the feds and the blacks, us fems were doing something in one part of the main house and Soul and the males were in another part. I was walking through to the male side when I stopped. There was Soul, with his shoulder-long hair and beard and that presence of his, surrounded by seven or eight dudes who were sort of leaning toward him, while Soul was looking at them in his calm, intense way, from one to the other, as if he was taking their measure, every one of them.

It was like a revelation: *Jesus and his apostles.*

Did I believe that Jesus Coyote was the second coming of Jesus Christ? I'm not sure of second coming. It is possible that there have been earlier "comings," both of the real and the demon Jesus. But, yes, I believed that he was, one way or another, Jesus. We all believed that. And if he had something of the devil to go along with the Jesus part—that was cool with us since we were fed up with the straight world.

Soul dug playing Jesus. Sometimes he'd even have us nail him up naked to a big wooden cross and look down on us while we orgied.

He would say: "I'm Jesus crucified. I will die for you. But will you die for me?"

I guess he was preparing us to murder for him.

He played Jesus but he also played Satan. Like he used to go on about this wide hole in the desert floor near Furnace Mountains. Soul called it Devil's Hole and kept repeating how he'd lead us through the hole once the bad shit came down and there was all-out war. What he thought was on the other side of his Devil's Hole—hell or heaven or some combination of the two—was never clear.

The bad shit Soul was always talking about toward the end was what he himself brought on. Sure the world is fucked up but it wasn't any worse the second year we were together than the year before that. But like I said, Soul was inventing things to get worked-up about. It's true, we had a lot more maroons in the tribe—as much as 70—when we were in Death Valley, and we were having trouble supporting everyone. Raiding the supermarket trash bins for veggie scraps wasn't going to cut it for 70 mouths to feed.

So we began to do other things, like steal credit cards and cars. We'd steal a car, then strip it, remove the engine and whatever other parts we needed and transport the hardware to the movie ranch or to Death Valley (we crashed in both places). Then the guys who were real good with mechanical stuff—Soul, Sarge, Donkey Don, Fang—would build dune buggies, which was pretty much how we got around in Death Valley. Soul even talked about mounting machine guns on the buggies and raiding the desert towns.

After a bunch of cars were reported stolen, the cops traced some of them, along with a few stolen credit cards, to us. Most of the tribe was at the movie ranch when the SWAT squad surprised us at dawn one Saturday and ordered us all outside. All the fems—like 35 of us—were lined up side-by-side, squatting on the ground, when Soul yipped like a coyote, which was our signal, and we all peed right there in front of the hard-boiled SWAT dudes. You know what? The SWATS didn't do anything to us. I still can't explain why. First I thought maybe they dug young pretty girls peeing. Then I thought for sure it was Soul's lucky star that kept us from getting our butts jailed. Soul must've been saving up all the bad luck for the shit that was to come down later.

I've heard some people say that the SWAT cops didn't arrest us because there was a conspiracy. CIA or some shit. The idea was that the cops encouraged Soul to get eviler and eviler so that they would have good reason to clamp down tight on maroons, on the counter-culture. Because we were that big a threat to so-called normal society.

I don't think I mentioned Cupid—Billy Sans-Soleil—a real handsome guy with a downy beard, a baby face and a huge dick. Cupid joined the tribe when we were already settled in LA and Death Valley. He was fascinated with the devil and starred in the underground movie *Satan in Tights*, a celebration of the devil and homosexuality, though Cupid himself was, like, the opposite of gay. As a teen, in Louisiana, where he was from, he was fucking his stepmother—and then when his father found out, he clubbed his father almost to death.

Cupid fucked almost as many girls as his master Coyote. Except Coyote fucked Cupid, the most hetero male imaginable, in the ass. After that, Coyote owned him. Which meant Coyote would end up sacrificing him, which he did by having Cupid kill Andy Hassler.

Andy was a studio musician, a real sweet gay dude. There was no reason to kill him at all.

The story the media ran with is that the Self and Gallo murders were copycat, with the same bloody scrawlings on the wall as at the Andy Hassler site. Soul's idea was that the police would think the real killers of Hassler and Self-Gallo were still at large and release Cupid. But that ain't the way it went down.

I was with Cupid when he murdered Andy, but I was against the murder and had nothing to do with it. It's true I told Soul that Andy had come into money, but that didn't mean I wanted to steal it from him or off him for it. Yes, I did scrawl a meaningless syllable, **RIX**, on the wall, but only because Soul ordered me to. What I'm saying is Soul was the one responsible for Andy Hassler's murder.

He came over to Andy's place and almost cut Andy's ear off with his machete. Then he ordered Cupid to finish him. Which makes it real ironic that the police would arrest me and Cupid for the crime.

Everyone gets on my case for talking too much, but it could be that if I didn't run my mouth about the Self-Gallo murders to my cellmate at Sybil Brand, Soul would still be out there doing his devil's work.

Andy Hassler, Bobby Steele, Naomi Self and her rich friends, the Gallo pair and probably a bunch of other people were murdered for one reason: Coyote's bloodlust. He instructed the tribe on how to use a seven-inch blade buck knife, how to penetrate the flesh, then twist the blade.

With the Self murders, he told Tex Embry what he wanted done and gave him the four knives. To me he just said: Use their blood to scrawl something witchy on the walls. So on the Self and Gallo walls I smeared the words **CRO** and **TOX.** I have no idea what they mean, I did it without thinking.

Do you know what Tex said to beautiful, pregnant Naomi just before he stuck the knife in her? "I am the devil and I'm here to do the devil's business." He meant that he was carrying out the assignment that Satan himself gave him.

Why did Soul choose to off Naomi Self and her rich friends? People said it was because he had a grudge against her husband, the Polish movie director, for something that happened at a party. Other people say it had to do with Don Fernando who was into S/M and maybe dissed Soul at a Hollywood orgy. People even say it had to do with Naomi Self, that Soul had balled her and then she rejected him.

All I know is Soul ordered me to kill and so I killed.

Meanwhile Soul claims to be paying the penalty for murders that he had no connection with. But it was all his idea, every little bit of it. When we came back from the Self murders, Tex told him what went down. What did Soul do? He went back to the house with Tex, moved the bodies around, put a towel over Don Fernando's face. Soul said later he was checking to see there were no fingerprints, which is a lie. He was just getting off on it, being in the massacre house with the butchered bodies while the blood was still warm.

Like the very next night, just after midnight, Soul gave us the cleaned-up buck knives and we went out again in the old Edsel—Soul, Tex, Bitch, Chong and me. Tex was driving. Except for Soul, we were all barefoot. People have commented that at both murders—Joya Grove and the Gallos—everyone was barefoot. Well, we were barefoot because of the clap. Everybody in the tribe was doing each other and so almost all of us got the Bangkok clap, which was the worst clap there was, the hardest to cure. Anyways, we didn't have the bread to buy antibiotics, so our feet swelled and it was real hard to wear shoes.

Soul directed us to the Gallo house and told us wait in the car. He got out, rang the bell, talked himself inside, then tied them up and gagged them. When he came out he said: "Do what you done yesterday." So we went in and murdered them. We all took part. Bette Mulder—Bitch—stuck the carving fork in Mr. Gallo's stomach and twanged it like a tuning fork. We stabbed them a bunch of times. In blood I smeared the words **CRO** and **TOX** on the walls. The whole deal took like an hour and a half.

Soul was waiting in the car when we got out. He had 300-mig Blue Unicorn tabs for all of us. We dropped the acid in the car, then took off our bloody clothes which we tossed in the trunk. Soul was driving and he stopped at a house in Bel Air and told us to use the water hose in the garden to clean off. We got out naked and washed each other with the hose, playing with the water and giggling like kids. We must have woke the owner up. He came out all mad and shit and tried to get the license number of the old Edsel. Tex had to knock him down, then we got in the car and took off.

Soul had brought some changes of clothing for us, so we got dressed in the car. By now the acid was kicking in big-time.

Soul asked us: "Is there anyone you know deserves killing?"

Chong chimed in: "I let this actor dude pick me up, we went back to his pad and fucked. He was all like stuck on himself, but you know what? He had a tiny cock and didn't even *bring* me. He deserves to die."

So we started to drive all the way to Venice Beach where tiny cock's pad was. On the way, Soul stopped at a Catholic Church, told us to wait in the car and went inside. Ten minutes later he was back out. He said he wanted to off a priest and hang him upside down on the cross by the altar, but he couldn't find one. They must be too busy sucking off little boys, Soul joked.

In Venice Beach, while Soul waited in the Edsel, Tex, Chong, Bitch and me, carrying the same buck knives we used on the Gallos, went up to tiny cock's pad on the second floor and knocked at the door. Nobody answered. My stomach started hurting, which sometimes happens with top-grade acid. So right there I raised my mini, squatted on the floor in front of tiny cock's pad, and took a smelly dump.

"It ain't the same as killing him," I said to Chong. "But it's better than nothing, right?"

We all laughed and skipped downstairs.

Later when Chong was trying to cop a plea, she said she deliberately led us to the wrong apartment because she didn't really want to kill tiny cock. That's a lie, and DA Dickerson didn't buy it. Chong is here in Frontera, in isolation just like me. I see her once a day at exercise, only she won't talk to me because of my grand jury testimony which I later retracted. She's a hypocrite, but Jesus says that even the vilest hypocrites and Pharisees are deserving of Christian love. I'm working on it.

One thing I haven't said anything about because it hurts so bad is my baby. I don't know for sure who the father was but I think it was Sarge, Bruce Keith. My baby was born in Death Valley, way premature—three months early—and weighed only four pounds. None of us were prepared, but as usual Soul took charge and knew just what to do. He bit off the umbilical chord, then used some gut from his guitar string to bind it. Soul said we should name the baby Abraxas-2, which is what we did. When I was arrested they took the baby from me and it was adopted by some people from Minnesota. That's what I heard anyways.

Soul always encouraged us to have babies to build up our numbers so that we could start a new race in his Devil's Hole. He himself fathered babies with Mercy, L'il Bess, GJ, Loca and a bunch of others outside the tribe. One thing that most people don't know is that Soul included the babies in the sex orgies. He would make us fondle and suck the infants—gentle of course. But it's not like the infants had any say in the matter. It was Soul's idea about what he called re-sexualizing a world that was being suppressed and puritanized. Young people sexing were less likely to become the kind of citizen-sheep that the mainstream culture demanded.

They say about Jesus—and I can testify to the truth of it—that just to say his name once in prayer releases a force which works in you even when you don't realize it.

I can't deny that Soul possessed some of that same force, even if it was designed for evil. That's why we shaved our heads and yipped like coyotes and gave ourselves Nazi tattoos and submitted totally to him. That's why when the SWAT team came after us in the movie ranch all the girls lined up, squatted on the ground and peed right in front of the cops. Even in isolation in prison we were in submission to Soul.

Like Hedda and Mercy—they're still in submission. They believe Soul's some kind of Godhead, even with all the horrible damage he's done.

Anyways, Soul has never forgave me. He was bummed that I testified for the grand jury even though I changed my mind and refused to cop a plea at the trial. People forget it was Li'l Bess, Donkey Don and Fang—Lamar Duane Cady—that ended up copping. Wasn't me.

You know what Soul is doing now? People, admirers, whatever, send him small gifts like socks or a shirt or sweater. What Soul does—and his wrists are shackled 24/7—is unravel them and make scorpions and dolls—voodoo dolls—out of them. Soul has always been real good with his hands. And this way—even though he's in supermax—he can still get back at his enemies.

It could be he sees me as one of his enemies, but I'm not worried. How much more can he do to me than he's already done? Besides, this black hole in me is filled to the brim with Jesus.

I want to say one last thing. People have accused me of fucking anything that moved. That's a lie. Like I never did Fang—Lamar Duane Cady—even in the orgies when everyone was with everyone. That's because he had an overbite. I never, ever liked dudes with overbites.

Jaroslav Hora
(19 years after, undisclosed location, Europe)

I made my mark early with ***Razors and Shadows****, which won the critics' prize at Venice.*

I was 25, two years younger than that *enfant terrible* Jean-Luc Godard was when he made *Breathless*. After my "triumph," obviously doors opened for me. But not absolutely. Most European producers, including the avant-garde French, were gun-shy about some of my more outlandish-seeming ideas.

Which is what brought me to America. In Hollywood outlandish films were welcomed so long as they were called "movies," contained a hefty dose of violence, had no big words, and "virtue" triumphed in the end. Moronic prescription, but not unsuitable to at least a few of my earlier filmic (movie) ideas. In *Night of the Thousand Knives*, for example, which was a great success in America, I finessed the American producers into thinking I was fulfilling their prescription, then deviated as I saw fit. They couldn't tell the difference.

Had I not gone to Hollywood I would not have met Naomi Self at the Disney-Nabisco "patio party" and would not have offered Naomi a role in *Vampire Daughters in Beverly Hills*. Although the American producers cut the film to shreds and I disowned it, it brought Naomi and me together, and set into motion the events at Joya Grove. If I had stayed in Europe or gone to Mexico like Buñuel, or to Japan like Wenders, Naomi, Viktor, Kristin and Don Fernando would not have been at Joya Grove. Presumably they'd all be alive as I am, nineteen years later. Instead, they were brutally, senselessly slaughtered and my life was shattered.

I was in London shooting *The White Devil*, with Jack Palance, when the news came. It was about 6 p.m., and several of us were in my Hampstead flat having cocktails. On the phone from LA was my American agent Davey Rose.

He said: "Jaro, I have terrible news."

I thought it might be his marriage which was chronically turbulent and about which he tended to talk incessantly. I remember sipping my gin and saying, "What's it this time, Davey?"

"The house on Joya Grove was devastated," he said. "Naomi, Viktor, Kristin, Don Fernando—they're all dead."

With that, my brain partially stopped functioning. Two words shot into my skull: *earthquake, landslide.*

"How is Naomi?" I asked senselessly.

There was a pause, then Rose blurted: "She's dead, Jaro. Murdered. They've all been murdered."

At that point I remember dropping the phone, falling onto my knees and banging my fists on the floor.

Meanwhile, Liam Fowler, my European agent, had picked up the phone and taken it into one of the other rooms.

My recollections of what happened after that are vague. I know that my British physician hurried over and injected me with a sedative. Liam arranged the Concorde flight to LA for the next day, and Liam and my doctor traveled with me. I was sedated during the flight and for much of the ten days I spent in LA, coloring that whole period with a weird hallucinatory sheen, which probably is as it should be in that psychotic fairyland. I did briefly discontinue the sedatives to take a lie detector test, which the LAPD informed me was standard procedure for crimes of a certain magnitude.

For the most part I was, as I indicated, in a semi-stupor, but as in a dream my mind kept coming back to a charming little scar that Naomi had on her left wrist from a carpal tunnel procedure she had five years before. It was the only scar on her otherwise perfect body and I was fixated on it, I can't explain why.

Naomi's funeral was the hardest part. She had been butchered even beyond the most gifted Hollywood mortician's art, and so her casket was kept closed. Her parents and younger sister were as broken up as I was. Her father, Kenyon Self, a tough-as-nails Special Forces colonel, gave the eulogy, breaking down twice in his delivery. Not even the sedatives prevented me from weeping uncontrollably for almost the entire service.

The services for Viktor and Don Fernando were easy by comparison. Kristin Barrett was buried in Connecticut, where she had been raised.

Because of the media feeding frenzy, I couldn't stay in my Malibu cottage, so a friend offered me his beach house in Santa Barbara. When the wealthy neighbors, none of whom was closer than fifty meters, heard that the infamous Jaroslav Hora was nearby they raised hell, claiming they were afraid of being savaged in their beds. After a few days of their bitching and moaning, another friend rented me a suite in the Murdoch Towers in Beverly Hills.

Hollywood is a hallucinatory place in the best of times, rank with gossip and bizarre rumors, but the mass murders of the stunningly beautiful pregnant actress wife of Hora and her friends on Joya Grove unleashed some unprecedented bitchiness, which the *LA Times* and other papers slavishly recorded.

While under the influence of LSD, Ecstasy and black magic, "hairstylist to the stars" Don Fernando was castrated and his genitals were stuffed into his gorgeous mistress Naomi Self's mouth.

Naomi Self's unborn child was ripped from the beautiful actress's womb and hanged from the rafters in the living room.

The mutilated victims, fitted with black execution hoods, were roped together and suspended upside down from the rafters.

The notorious movie director Jaroslav Hora's name was smeared in blood on his beautiful dead wife's stomach after the fetus was ripped out.

On and on. The LAPD chief detectives with whom I was in close touch informed me that none of the above was even remotely true. It was a bloody massacre, and the victims were stabbed many, many times, but there was no sexual mutilation, the fetus—our child—was intact, and none of the bloody scrawls mentioned my name.

Two strange words, or syllables: **CRO** and **TOX**, were smeared in blood on the walls. The victims' heads were not hooded; the coroner, after his preliminary examination, covered Don Fernando's head with a towel because the multiple knife thrusts in his upper neck had exposed brain matter.

Nonetheless, the national media picked up on these cruel rumors and treated them as factual,

According to *People*, the "Hora set" was known as the kinkiest in Hollywood, featuring heavy, indiscriminate drug users and jaded orgiasts, who routinely picked up brutal bikers and other unsavory characters, supplied them with dope and invited them to orgies at the Joya Grove mansion.

Time opted for a "ritual mock execution under the influence of hallucinogens that got out of hand," with the celebrants ending up mutilating and murdering each other.

Newsweek hit on two findings at the house: a Ouija board and a video of Naomi and Hora "having sex" to launch its speculations of depravity, black magic, and ritual murder.

I wonder whether you can imagine the emotional agony these character assassinations, none with a grain of sympathy for the victims, flung me into. Especially since the paparazzi in the US and Europe would not ease up on me any time of the day or night.

Some people expressed surprise that with all the emotional turmoil I felt, I mounted my own investigation of the massacre. The truth is that I acted on a suggestion from LAPD Detective Vince Edwards. Not that Edwards was encouraging me to compete with the special task force; rather he asked me to try to recall threats and other hostile actions, especially by acquaintances. When I cited several such instances, Edwards in effect recommended that I do some private sleuthing and report any findings to him.

At that stage of the investigation, law enforcement's best guess was that the murderers were spurned or aggrieved acquaintances with connections to international drug distribution.

I did not find that theory convincing. And despite my quasi-stupor induced by the sedatives, I was at the same time strangely hyper, determined to contribute to the investigation. I received permission to visit the crime scene on Joya Grove, not because of my so-called preoccupation with blood and gore and not because I wanted to snatch the pornographic videos. There was just the one video of Naomi and me making love which I had recorded to try out a camera I was using on the set, and that video had been confiscated. Contrary to rumors, there were no porn videos of Hollywood actors and actresses. My motive in returning to the massacre scene was to see whether the police might have missed something potentially significant.

Accompanied by Det. Edwards, I went to the Joya Grove house which was cordoned off, and except for the removed bodies and what the police had confiscated as possible evidence, it was as it had been after the massacre: much dried blood and viscera in the vicinity of the murders, including a thick, uneven trail of blood leading to the path where the boy visiting the grounds-keeper was murdered in his sports car.

Maybe because I was under sedation, or because of the lingering shock, I felt less pent-up and emotional than I'd expected. I examined the bloody **CRO** and **TOX** scrawled on the walls. I walked through the various rooms: Naomi's bedroom, where she was lying in our canopied bed and talking with Don Fernando; another bedroom in the east wing where Kristin Barrett was in bed reading a new translation of Kafka's *Amerika* I had recommended and was considering filming; the living room where Viktor was dozing on a Regency sofa. I looked through the four guest bedrooms, each of the five bathrooms, the sauna, and the two spas. I examined the kitchen, pantry, dining room, and maid's quarters.

With Det. Edwards' permission, I removed an item of lingerie from Naomi's bedroom drawer, a mauve teddy that was among the things I had bought for her last birthday. Then we left.

Note: The media have confused this visit to Joya Grove with my return to LA in December at the request of the District Attorney. When I revisited Joya Grove in December it was with a psychic named Cassandra. She was well-recommended (though by Hollywood acquaintances, who are far from the best judges in those matters). In any case, she claimed to feel strong "vibes," and cadged some intimate photos I'd taken of Naomi. She then sold the photos to a weekly tabloid and disappeared. She was, in a word, a swindler who'd calculated correctly that I would be too bereft to prosecute her.

Edwards' suggestion that I think in terms of friends, acquaintances and hangers-on jogged my memory back to the birthday party I put together for Naomi—her 27th birthday—just before I left for London to shoot *The White Devil*. We had the party on Joya Grove with lots of invitees. And as usual in so-called famous parties, there were gate-crashers. In this instance, three seedy-looking humans—two males and a female—arrived together and immediately began to make a nuisance of themselves. I myself gave the order that they be forcibly ejected, which is what the two bodyguards, assisted by my friend Viktor Hus, did. On his way out of the door, one of the crashers shouted some kind of violent threat over his shoulder.

As it turned out, the crashers were traced and each of the three had an airtight alibi which excluded them from suspicion.

I didn't stop there. Belladonna, the male lead singer of the metal band Toxic, had broken up with his gorgeous wife Celine who escaped to Amsterdam and was consorting with the massively endowed Dutch porn star, Hans-14. Not only that, soon after her flight, Celine and Hans-14 had allowed themselves to be videotaped having sex, and those steamy sessions were widely viewed on the porn circuit.

Belladonna was an ex-circus knife-thrower known for his terrible temper, and he was taking the betrayal hard, making noises about cutting up the two lovers. In better times Celine and Belladonna and Naomi and I would occasionally party together. And before I left for London to shoot *The White Devil* Celine and I had a passionate one-night-stand in a suite in the Beverly Hills Marriott, heightened by some of the best, purest X I'd ever done. I couldn't help wondering if, in their most recent spat, she had mentioned the fling to Belladonna and if he then exacted vengeance on my wife and her friends.

Far-fetched as my suspicions might seem, I decided to contact Celine through acquaintances in Amsterdam and ask her. Her answer was yes, she had mentioned our one-night-stand to Belladonna and he hadn't taken it well. She also said in passing (I didn't confide to her my suspicions) that Belladonna was in the LA area during the time of the murder.

My next step—this time without the blessings of the LAPD—was to find out when Belladonna and his band were on the road and, with the assistance of a professional burglar who came highly recommended, I disarmed Belladonna's alarm system and broke into his garage in Bel Air. I took samples from Belladonna's Jaguar and Rolls and had them tested for blood. The results were negative.

I still wasn't absolutely convinced. The next night, I broke into his house. I knew that he kept a journal—had in fact seen his Gucci black leather journal in his house once when the four of us met there. I wasn't sure how often he wrote in it. And I hoped that he hadn't taken it with him while touring. I found the journal in a bedroom drawer.

What struck me at once as I leafed through the pages was that the entire text was printed in block letters and that the words seemed to bear a likeness to the **TOX** and **CRO** that were printed in blood on the walls. Moreover, **TOX** could have been an allusion to Toxic, the name of Belladonna's band.

Back in my hotel I read through the journal and found neither my name nor Naomi's name. The next morning I took the journal and police photos of the bloody scrawls to one of the handwriting experts that Det. Edwards had mentioned. The expert said that his best estimate was that the scrawls and journal entries were not made by the same hand, then demonstrated some of the subtle differences in the lettering. He quickly added that his opinion was provisional because the block letters and the blood made it impossible to make an accurate assessment.

This almost excluded Belladonna from my consideration, but not quite. With the aid of the LAPD, I got myself wired. Then I made it a point to interview several of my acquaintances, including Belladonna, whom I saw soon after his band returned from Seattle. We met for a drink at the RKO Hilton. Evidently Belladonna wasn't aware that his house had been broken into or that his journal was missing; at least he didn't mention it.

He greeted me with much sympathy and no trace of resentment. He said further that Celine had tired of her tryst with Hans-14 and was returning home; all was forgiven. We parted on friendly terms. Still, I recommended that the LAPD give him a lie detector test, which they subsequently did and which he passed without ambiguity.

Probably I should have waited for the result of the lie detector test before deciding whether to investigate Belladonna, but sedated as I was I felt an odd compulsion to take things into my own hands.

After Belladonna, I recorded Eddy Eagle, the actor-martial arts expert who had a crush on Naomi but was spurned in my favor. Like Belladonna, Eddy Eagle was known for his temper and was routinely booked for assault or disorderly conduct. Eddy Eagle seemed considerably affected by the massacre and said several times that he wished he were present in Joya Grove to break the necks of the would-be murderers. Instead, he was, he said, in Hong Kong shooting a movie with Bruce Lee. This was later confirmed.

I also recorded a few other people in our "set" who seemed suspicious and turned over the results to Edwards. None turned out to be implicated.

Appalling as the murders and their aftermath were, it has to be said that those two and a half years that Naomi and I loved each other and were together were the only times before or since that I've actually been happy. Almost deliriously happy.

Would I have agreed to a Faustian exchange: two-and-a-half years of delirious joy for a lifetime of depression, regret and impotent rage? From this perspective nineteen miserable years later, I'd have to say no. But were I asked then, in 1969, I might have replied otherwise.

Regarding what I called my impotent rage, I must deny the accusations of the maniac Coyote's cult that I put out a "contract" on Coyote while he was at Corcoran State Prison. I don't deny I was bitterly disappointed when his death sentence was commuted because of some absurd technicality. I would have liked to see the filthy alpha wolf and his murderous tribe-clones—Bakramp, Embry, Cheech, Mulder, all of them—die in agony like their victims on Joya Grove, but it was not my business to ensure that that happened.

Rather than putting out a contract on Coyote, someone—likely Coyote himself—ordered his tribe-goons that were not locked up to terrorize and even to assassinate me. Three times, a witch's brew of viscera and evil-smelling filth was left on my doorstep in Malibu, where I lived briefly while the trial was going on. And when I moved back to Paris there were at least two attempts on my life that I would attribute to Coyote. Which is why I have been living in an undisclosed location in Europe with round-the-clock protection.

What I've characterized as a satanic antagonism to me, is—as colleagues have pointed out—banally ironic. Because it was the extraordinary popularity of my own film *Night of the Thousand Knives* that seems to have launched a broadly based interest in satanism and witchcraft. Americans who previously couldn't distinguish Lucifer from Richard Nixon were suddenly getting worked up about the demonic and the supernatural. So my getting hassled by witches brews, and the Joya Grove massacre itself, were in fair part provoked by my successful film. That's what it means to get hoisted by one's own petard.

Another major annoyance I've had to put up with is the comparison people in and out of the media insist on making between maniac Coyote and me. We're both "diminutive," we're both highly sexed, we've both experimented with mind-altering drugs, we share an interest in horror and the supernatural, and each of us was, so to speak, granted two-and-a-half glorious years surrounded on either side by bleakness. For me, the glory was my relationship with Naomi and our unborn son in her belly, along with a burst of creativity that I have not experienced since. For Coyote it was his accumulation of hippie disciples, orgies, drugs and moronic philosophizing, crowned by the savage mass murders. On either side of his hallucinatory two-and-a-half years were the thirty or forty prisons where he spent his life both before and since.

I'm a European-Jewish award-winning filmmaker whose grandparents on my father's side were gassed in the Nazi camps, and I've been known to make serious films which are sometimes bloody. Coyote is an illiterate, anti-Semitic mass murdering hillbilly with a swastika tattoo between his eyes who has spent virtually his entire life in prison.

Where, please enlighten me, is the similarity?

I've been asked countless times whether Coyote harbored a grudge against me. I never met him, of that I am certain. So if he disliked or hated me it would have to be based on my films or on media accounts of me.

The same question has been asked regarding Naomi, and my response is I am certain that Naomi never met the maniac. I cannot speak for my friend

Viktor Hus or for Don Fernando, but I'm doubtful there as well simply because they traveled in very different circles. Sure, we all went to Hollywood-type parties, but I can't recall ever seeing a filthy barefoot Coyote cult "maroon" at any of them.

According to Det. Edwards and my own investigations, Coyote did have a few flaky contacts in the entertainment industry, including a well-known male actor who was a closet homosexual and whom Coyote serviced for money. But virtually no one in the industry took him seriously or wanted in any way to associate with him. Coyote was supposed to be a singer and song writer, and evidently he bullied the drummer in the Beach Boys to listen to his bilge. He even managed to persuade the Beach Boys to record a few of his creations on one of their LP's before they broke off relations with him.

I actually forced myself to hear one of his home-made records; the singing and acoustic guitar strumming were amateurish-bordering-on-incompetent. And the songs themselves were, as I said, bilge, utterly simple-minded.

For the police, as I said, the motive for the Joya Grove massacre from the outset had to do with drugs. But almost everyone young and famous in Hollywood did (and does) drugs and so the police found drugs in the house. It is possible that Don Fernando supplied some of his wealthy clientele with coke or hash, but he was in no way a big-time drug dealer. And I can't believe that Victor was a major player in smuggling MDMA from Europe or Israel. Viktor already had plenty of money from an inheritance and was engaged to the Phillip Morris heiress Kristin Barrett who was worth millions. The fact is that Viktor was singularly uninterested in anything that resembled work. He was an indolent charmer, among the laziest people I'd ever known.

My opinion finally is the Joya Grove massacre was an arbitrary mass murder at the instigation of the insane guru Coyote, probably to reinforce his power-mania. Regarding the murder of the Gallos the next night, I heard that there had been some previous interaction between Coyote and "Mambo Joe" Gallo, but that is as much as I can say here.

As far as the conspiracy theorists' notion that Coyote was set up by the FBI and DEA to justify harsh official measures against the "counter-culture," I can't buy it. For one thing, I don't believe that the FBI and DEA are competent enough to successfully organize an undercover operation on that level.

Until Joya Grove both Naomi and I felt well disposed to the so-called counter-culture. We approved of young people trying to get close to nature, loving each other, experimenting with psychoactive drugs, shunning material ambitions. Since Coyote and his communal cult, I see that I was wrong. As Hobbes and others have argued, humans in their natural state tend to do evil and are fundamentally corrupt. They need the chains and restraints that official culture imposes on them to be forcibly separated from their brutal primal selves.

Even now, nearly twenty years later, when I see a kid with moony eyes and filthy hair aping the maroon style, my mind is jolted back to those images of Coyote and his cult, and I feel the bile mount to my throat. It is fortunate that I am forbidden to carry a knife or pistol. I would be sorely tempted to murder these swinish counter-culture creatures on sight.

I began to have sex about a month after Naomi's death, soon after returning to London. I was a famous, or infamous, director. It was known that I liked girls and knew what to do with them. Moreover, my connection to the Hollywood massacre seemed to make me even more desirable. In a word, females were everywhere around me and I took full advantage of my opportunities in an attempt to forget the brutal murder of the person I loved most in the world. The promiscuous sex was mostly with very young girls, who seemed to like me particularly, and whom, in the aftermath of the massacre, I preferred sexually. The sex was often fueled by hashish or X, and managed temporarily to relieve my mind of my misery. But inevitably it would come back to haunt me all over again.

I continue to make films, obviously, and I am still considered by the *cognoscenti* a gifted film director. But I sometimes feel that I am working by rote. The spirit of discovery and play that I felt as a director before the massacre—that, sad to say, is long gone.

Sweetheart, *Cherie, Cara, Liebling.* Naomi, darling, however I might act in this unforgiving world, there is only you and there will always be only you.

Cupid
(18 year after, Folsom State Prison)

Call me motherfucker.

Well, *stepmotherfucker*, so maybe that ain't as bad. Isn't there a myth where the father remarries a much younger woman that tries to seduce her stepson but is rejected? What happens is the spurned stepmother tells the father that his son tried to seduce *her* and the furious old man castrates the kid.

Well, my old man remarried a much younger woman who had a look at me, liked what she saw, and went after it. I was only 13 but kids mature real fast where I came of age—Terrebonne Parish, Louisiana. In the bayou the two dominants are sex and food. Like my uncle Maxime was such a good cook that he could take your left shoe and turn it into a Cajun barbecue orgy.

But I wasn't into eating. My thing was girls, and young as I was had already fucked me a baker's dozen. Like I'm sure my stepmother, who was probably in her mid-thirties, expected a virgin. I know she expected a scared kid she could seduce and master. I knew it even then and at the start I played that role for her benefit. I was afraid that if I didn't play passive she would change her mind and not come after me.

Did she turn me on? Well, that was long before I found Jesus, okay? I was thirteen, hung and horny. Super-horny. Any female younger than seventy-nine was going to bulge my jeans. But I have to say that my stepmother was kind of sexy in her own right: slender with lots of wavy dyed auburn hair, a long back and fine tapering ass. She had small firm titties and tiny stickout pink nipples, sort of like some of the teenage girls I was fucking.

Her name was Chase, from Philadelphia. She was supposed to be upper class, but for some reason didn't have much money. Which is why she married my father, who was the opposite of upper class but had made a lot of jack from his construction company. He was a widower—my real mom died of cancer when I was in second grade—who must've been in his late fifties when he married Chase. The old man was sort of a raunchy looking Creole, but with his prosperity he cleaned himself up in an attempt to look civilized. It didn't work, he looked like an ape in a fancy suit. And Chase must've not liked apes in suits because she didn't seem to dig his raunchy ass at all. She dug me.

I said the old man was Creole. He was a mixture of French, Scotch-Irish, Choctaw and black and he was born smack-dab in the Louisiana bayou. My real mom was bona fide redneck trailer-trash from South Carolina. They met when my dad was in Marine Corps boot camp at Parris Island. I don't have any brothers or sisters. They wanted to have more kids but because of her medical problems my mom couldn't deliver after me. I think that was always an issue between them. My dad came from a large family and he wanted a brood of kids but my mom just couldn't come through. I know the old man was fucking on the side even when my mom was alive.

I never cared what they did or didn't do. From the start I was the kind of kid that nothing really bothered me. I was absorbed in my own pleasures and that was it. I had a baby face but was well built with an unusually large cock and I never got tired of looking at myself naked in the mirror and jacking off.

Now Chase—she flashed me sexy looks and I either pretended not to notice or to be embarrassed, the way an adolescent kid would be. What I really wanted was for her to make the first move and let's jambalaya. She finally made her move about three weeks or so after my old man brought her home with him from Philly and proudly introduced her as his new wife.

It was Monday bloody Monday, the shittiest day of the week needless to say. I came home from school at three o'clock and was surprised to find Chase's sunflower yellow Mustang parked outside. Usually she was out shopping or gambling in one of the reservations. This time she was home taking a bath. She pretended she didn't hear me come in and walked out of the bathroom nude.

"Oh Billy," she said with fake irritation. "I didn't hear you come in."

She didn't cover herself up with her arms or go back in the bathroom. She just stood there with her hands on her hips glaring at me, like I'd done something wrong.

I pretended to blush while checking her out.

Like I said, she had that long sweet curve of the hip. And the firm titties with the tiny pink stickout nipples. Her pussy hair was light brown, fine and smooth like a young girl's. She had long arms and delicate small hands and feet. Her dyed auburn hair was stacked high on her head so that I could see her swan neck.

"This is the time I always come home from school, Mom."

Still with her hands on her hips, with her hips pushed forward and that make-believe angry look, she said: "Do you like having me as a step-mom, Billy?"

"Uh-huh."

"Is that all you can say? 'Uh-huh'?"

"I love having you as a step-mom, Mom."

"What do you love about it, son?"

"What I love about it is you're so doggone purty."

"You think I'm pretty, don't you Billy?" Now she had moved her hands up to her hair and was staring at the big bulge in my fly.

"Yes'm."

"You think I'm sexy too, don't you, son?"

"Yes'm."

"You know what, Billy, since you think I'm so pretty and sexy I'm going to make you prove it."

Next thing we were in each other's arms and then on the floor, which is where I did her that first time and a bunch of times after that. Despite her talking stern and all that, she liked me to treat her rough, hold her wrists down hard while I was fucking her. Or if I was doing her from the back, pull her hair, bite her neck a little. Nothing real extreme. I didn't give a shit. Rough, smooth, in between, I dug every damn little bit of it.

Well, everything good has to come to an end. At least that's what they say. The only exception being my love for Jesus. My step-mom Chase and I were humping for eight or nine months, and the longer we did it the cockier we became and the more chances we took. Like she'd be in bed with the old man and when he was asleep and snoring she'd come into my room to fuck.

One night my father either pretended to sleep or was sleeping then woke up. Whatever it was, he followed her into my room and found us there in *flagrante delicto*.

The old fuck switched on the light and glared at his naked wife and naked son with his eyes bulging out. Next he started to sputter and spit and I could see by his reddening face that his blood pressure was shooting way up. Then he turned real fast out of the room, and I was thinking *gun*. Naked, with my stiff dancing cock, I hopped out of bed, grabbed a baseball bat (a heavy Willy McCovey model) from my closet, and followed him. He'd already taken the 6-inch barrel Ruger .357 out of the drawer in his bedroom and was about to open the box of rounds when I came at him with the bat. I had to hit him twice before he went down, on the side of his head and on the top of his head. Even then he was down but not out. I swung with both hands pretty much as hard as I could and hit him a third time on his forehead and top of his nose. This time he was out and squirting lots of blue-black blood from his nose.

I picked up the Ruger and box of rounds and returned to my room where my step-mom was cowering on the bed, the covers pulled up to her nose. I slipped into my jeans and a t-shirt, grabbed my leather jacket from the closet, and said: "I'm hitting the highway, Mom. Lend me some money, okay?"

"You didn't kill him, did you, Billy?"

"I reckon I didn't. But I ain't gonna hang around to find out either."

"My purse is in the living room. Take what you want."

I blew her a kiss, got the money out of her purse along with her car keys and cigs, and split. I was feeling strangely calm, not at all uptight for having just done an Oedipus—fucked my mom and maybe killed my old dad.

I slid into Chase's sunflower yellow Mustang convertible, lit one of her Salems, slipped the Ruger and rounds under the passenger seat and took off heading west, the vast sweet world moist and open before me.

Long story short: the police picked me up outside Houston before I had a chance to shoot some bad person or even get my nut. I was lectured by the judge about the evils of fucking your stepmother, batting around your father, and copping his Ruger .357. Then I was sentenced to five years in the Parchman Boys' Camp, a kind of military reform school deal, in Natchez, Mississippi, for criminal offenders ages 12 to 18.

Now hold your fire, it wasn't all that bad. Some of the older, harder kids had cool ideas about raising hell and making easy money that I was able to use when I got out four years later. While I was inside I had my first sexual experiences with boys. Well, not exactly first. I let myself be sucked off back home every once in a while. Anyway, in Parchman I was very popular because of my looks and my dancing big cock. I can tell you with all honesty that I never got on my knees, but I did get blown a lot and I did me some cornholing.

When they let me out early for good behavior I had just turned eighteen. And, no, my spirit wasn't broken. On the contrary, I felt raunchier and more defiant than ever. Oh yeah, a few months before I was set to get out Chase wrote that my old dad had dropped dead of a massive heart attack. She asked if she could visit me here in the slam. I never answered her.

Someone once said this but it bears repeating:

Fucking your mom is cool but finite.

Okay, I'm out with an old suitcase in my hand in Natchez, Mississippi. If I was black I'd be singing the blues. But I only have about one-sixth black in me, just enough to account for my dancing big cock. I hitch a ride west out of that KKK armpit before I even have a cup of coffee.

One of the experienced kids in Parchman told me the easiest bread for a dancing cock like mine was hustling homos. Which is what I did in Houston with great success. When I accumulated fifteen hundred dollars—which didn't take that long—I bought a used fire engine-red Camaro convertible and continued driving west. My idea was to go to Hollywood and become a movie star. Like Travolta in *Saturday Night Fever*, only without the faggy dancing. There was only one part of me that danced, and that was the way I liked it.

No, I didn't have a driver's license, insurance, any of that shit. I drove with the top down and the radio on real loud and picked up hitchhiking girls and even dudes. Driving from Houston to LA I think I picked up six girls and banged every one of them either in the car or outside off the road. The dudes—I let one of them blow me for jack. I smoked weed in the car. I even dropped acid—200 migs of Orange Sunshine—and still drove. I was taking a big chance, right? Know what? I was never once stopped by the ***po***lice. Call it luck. When you have it, ride it. I had it then and for maybe three or four years after that—then it all went south.

I had names of people that lived in Santa Fe, New Mexico, so I stopped off there. I made a few calls and they weren't in. So I split. I didn't like the dry climate. I'm a bayou guy, remember?

Well, the Camaro started to cough. It gave out just east of Phoenix and I had to ditch it. I could see there was hustling jack to be made in Phoenix, but it looked like a plastic place and way too hot and dry for me. I hitched the rest of the way to LA.

It took me a while to get used to how spread out LA was, but once I did everything fell into place. For a while I lived with this older movie producer in Bel Air. He dug me so much that he agreed to my terms: In return for sucking my dancing big cock, he paid me nice $$, gave me room and board in his fancy house, bought me a new Camaro, and introduced me to movie people.

After I was given a screen test that came out good, I picked up a few minor roles in teen sun and surf flicks. But nothing big seemed to be in the offing from the mainstream side. Then I met Dick Diver, a well-known gay, off-beat movie director, at a patio party my sugar daddy gave. He asked to see my cock, and I reckon he liked what he saw because he made an offer to me straight-up: I star in an x-rated film he was planning to shoot about Satan. Yeah, the devil. Dick Diver belonged to one of those weird cults that were everywhere in the LA area. His particular deal had originated in England and combined a sort of gothic S/M gay sex with devil-worship.

As soon as I agreed to star in that devil flick I struck a chord that would vibrate for the rest of my life. It was that movie that Soul saw and it enforced our connection to each other. It's a weird thing, because on the surface me being offered this starring role would seem to represent the best break I had so far, but in the long term it laid the groundwork for all the evil shit I would become involved with through my affiliation with Soul. Like an earthquake set into motion with the earth shifting, but it doesn't erupt until much later.

To make it more complicated: if there was no devil-worship movie there might not have been Coyote and this life sentence I've been serving in Folsom, but there definitely would not have been Jesus. Which means there would not have been Billy San-Soleil's ministry for Christ. The hell I was in moved me through Coyote up to Jesus. That's how I've come to see it anyway.

So I got the starring role in Dick Diver's *Satan in Tights*, and the acting wasn't hard at all. I was naked through most of it and so I pretty much did my thing. My dancing big cock—even with all the lights and technicians and interruptions on the set—responded like it always did. The only slightly hard thing was I had to learn some Latin words in order to mock God and praise Lucifer. I enjoyed the work, enjoyed the sex, and enjoyed the payoff, $25,000, plus royalties.

They say you can never be too hung or too rich. Well I had the hung side covered, and the 25k with royalties was a pretty good start on the jack side. I left my sugar daddy and moved to a duplex in Laurel Canyon with two sexy girls, Charlene and Lori. Pretty soon Lori's friend Emma moved in, so I was fucking three girls, usually two or three at a shot. Jesus wasn't in my life yet, but it was a real sweet time, I have to say. We did the hottest drugs on the black market, and one Saturday my three girls and me each dropped 250 migs of Blue Unicorn—the best acid available.

As often happens when I drop acid, I got a hankering for *escargot*, so me and my fems popped into a trendy French restaurant in Hollywood without a reservation. A C-note slipped to the maître d' got us a choice table.

Guess who we saw? Naomi Self and Jaroslav Hora with another pair. They were sitting at a big table to our left, surrounded by palms and greenery. But Naomi Self and me—we were right in line. We could look into each other's eyes without anyone else noticing.

I was wearing very tight, soft, black leather pants, Jim Morrison style, with my dancing big cock snaking down my thigh. I stood up and stretched so that Naomi could check me out, and she liked what she saw. She looked over at me all through dinner, with a flirty little smile on her face. Spearing my *escargots*, I thought to myself: How do I get to that sweet puss? Once I got her alone fucking her would not be a problem, trust me.

Hora meanwhile was doing all the talking. With the piped-in music I couldn't hear him but I could see his crooked little mouth moving animatedly. He was wearing some kind of Fauntleroy outfit, with a frilly collar and cuffs. I didn't like his manner at all and I wondered what super-sexy Naomi could possibly see in him. Cocky as he presented himself, I seriously doubted he knew how to fuck or had much yardage down there. He called himself a "serious" film-maker and got lucky with his *Night of the Thousand Knives*, which won some awards. Me, I didn't think it was all that good a flick.

Sure, I'm sorry that Naomi Self was murdered the way she was, but I never was able to feel anything for Hora. I guess that shows I'm not as Christian as I'd like to be. What can I say?

I was a ladies' man, right?, so my ears always pricked up when I heard something cool about the ladies. People I knew, dopers in and around the offbeat movie scene, were talking about a little guy, an ex-con, some kind of guru who called himself Soul and had thirty or forty beautiful young girls following him like lemmings. Supposedly, they were dividing their time between a ghost town near the Funeral Mountains in Death Valley and a movie ranch in the Santa Susana Mountains, and they traveled around in a large black bus that was outfitted like a harem. The girls didn't wear shoes or underwear under their sheer long dresses, and when Soul, the pint-sized guru, strummed his guitar they would link hands and dance like dervishes twirling their dresses up around their naked hips. Then they would orgy and the little guru would do every last one of 'em.

Fucking forty girls in a single session—that takes stamina. I knew my dancing big cock had the zest but I doubted anyone else did. That's how cocky and arrogant I was then before Jesus entered my life and humbled me.

Needless to say, I was real curious, so I thought I would take the Camaro and my three girls and scoot out to the Harker movie ranch, where I was told they were camping, since it was August and too hot to be anywhere near Death Valley.

I'd heard about the movie ranch even before Soul and his harem because it was the site for a shitload of westerns—Gary Cooper, Duke Wayne, Audie Murphy, Randolph Scott—all those famous old guys shot cowboy movies there. My impression was it had gotten pretty run-down but that there were horses people could rent out for the day. Old man Harker, who was supposed to be almost blind, still lived on the premises.

We started out about nine-thirty on a Monday morning in early August and got to Chatsworth in the Simi Hills about an hour later. From there we drove about five miles northeast and turned into the ranch. I pulled the Camaro right next to a partially boarded-up saloon which still had a rusted-out name over the swinging doors: **Silver Spurs**, probably a left-over from the last western shot there.

I said before that I didn't like hot, dry places, but since I came to LA my feelings about that changed somewhat. Maybe it was all that good dope. Anyhow, the Harker ranch was even better than I expected. Slim sexy girls, some topless, gliding around, exercising the horses, sitting cross-legged on the ground and sewing. Two of them were bathing each other in a big old wooden bucket. When they saw us pull up a few of the girls smiled while the others just continued what they were doing.

Suddenly—and this was real unusual for me—I wasn't sure what my next move should be. And it was at that moment that I saw the little guru himself, Soul, walking toward us apparently from one of the outbuildings. He moved like an animal—a wolf, or a coyote—lightly on the balls of his feet, but with something wild held in reserve. He had shoulder-length black hair and a full black beard and he was smiling at us, a kind of radiant smile, even though his black eyes were unblinking, fixed. He wore a white, collarless East Indian-style blouse, simple gray workpants and rope sandals.

He walked over to the Camaro and in a soft even voice said: "Welcome. Come on out and have a look."

We all got out of the Camaro and followed him.

Motioning to various ramshackle outbuildings, he said: "Where we sleep."

I saw that behind the farthermost building was a circular grassy space and that the grass had been tended to. It looked like a small arena but with some kind of altar setup at one end.

"Where we play," Soul said, referring to the grassy area.

Actually, I wasn't sure if he said "play" or "pray." Lori said later that she'd heard "pray," but Emma and Charlene heard "play."

Walking back toward the Camaro, he turned left toward the stables. I saw four girls shoveling and sweeping horse shit.

"Work," Soul said.

Suddenly he stopped and turned toward Charlene who was separated by a few yards from my two other girls.

"Do you like to ride, Charlene?"

We were all taken aback because no one had mentioned any names. How would he know she was Charlene?

Charlene sputtered some kind of response and Soul laughed out loud. When we got to the saloon, he said, "Where we eat. When you come next time you'll eat with us."

Then he raised his hand in a wave, or benediction, turned his back and walked away. Again, several of the pretty half naked "tribe" girls looked up at us. And I saw two slim young males, barechested, moving a large wooden table out of the saloon in the direction of the outbuildings.

We got into the Camaro for the drive back. My girls were impressed.

Lori said: "How did he know your name, Charlene?"

"No clue," Charlene said.

"He's cool," Emma said.

"Whole setup's cool," Lori said.

I noticed they were talking softly, almost meditatively. Something of the atmosphere had already influenced them. Through my work on *Satan in Tights* I'd met a lot of self-styled devil worshippers. Some were game players, phonies, but others seemed to have an authentic vibe of one kind or other. I'd spent time in the church when I was young. My old man was Catholic and my real mom was Pentecostal. I couldn't make out whether the powerful quiet vibes Soul gave off were Satanic or Christ-like.

What I knew for damn sure was I'd be going back.

When we got back to the duplex we dropped 300 migs of Orange Sunshine and fucked and it was even better than usual. My three girls were naked with me on the rug and just as I was about to penetrate Charlene, Soul whispered into my ear: *Do her ass, Cupid.*

So I rubbed some spit on my dancing big cock and thrust into her asshole. I'd done Lori and Emma that way but not Charlene who was afraid of it. Not this time. She gave off a loud pleasurable groan—almost a growl—from deep in her chest.

In the acid vision Soul had called me Cupid, which was the name folks would know me by from that time on.

My three girls and I revisited Harker's movie ranch again the following Saturday, this time in the early evening. We ate dinner with the tribe—about 30 girls and six guys, including Soul, sitting at the head of the table—in the saloon, with its weird movie-set bar and winding stairs. We passed around wooden bowls with brown rice and veggies, corn tortillas. Baked apple filled with tahini for dessert. Everything fresh and tasty.

Then we moved to the grassy arena, where a movie screen had been erected at one end. As we settled on to the grass, I wondered what we were in for. But there was no way I could have anticipated *Satan in Tights*.

Meanwhile joints were being passed around, top-grade weed. So there I was, Cupid Sans-Soleil with my dancing big cock on the big screen. I said that I liked getting naked, looking in the mirror and jacking off. Shit, this was even better, with beautiful girls on every side of me. Even as the movie was playing, with the sound track turned very low, everyone was getting naked. And then Soul, who'd been on the other side of the arena, was suddenly there with us, naked, embracing Charlene. I thought: Whoa! He's a fast-moving little guru.

By now the circle of naked girls and dudes had gotten tighter and people were doing each other. I was doing one side of Emma while she was doing one of the tribe girls. Then I changed position and slid my dancing cock in the vicinity of a few of the sweet tribe girls. At the same time, I had one eye on Soul who, sure enough, was fucking Charlene in the ass. I was cool with that, but his next move took me by surprise: he separated me from the tribe girl and while he was doing Charlene from behind, he began to suck my cock. Damn! He knew how to do it too. But that wasn't all. He shifted position so that I would suck his cock fresh from Charlene's ass. Now that was something I'd never, ever done or even considered doing. You know what? I did it, I even swallowed the heavy salty load that Soul shot into my mouth.

And I dug it.

Well, that may be an exaggeration. The image in my head as I swallowed his hot spew was my baptism when I was four or five years old. My mom's brother Damon, a Pentecostal preacher, immersed me in the bayou and I came up with a mouth full of brine and Jesus.

From that moment on, I was marked, a Coyote maroon, part of the tribe. I learned later that for Soul there were no sexual prohibitions: everybody did everybody else in every hole. That was one of the conditions for belonging to the tribe.

What happened next was I gave up my sweet Laurel Canyon condo, donated my entire savings account to Soul and moved in with the tribe.

Charlene and Lori came with me. Emma, for her own reasons, didn't. I also gave up my acting career. At the time those sacrifices didn't seem like sacrifices. I felt happy and at the same time protected. Hell, I didn't know that I needed to feel protected, I'd always been a carefree mo'fucker. But once under Soul's wing, it seemed like protection was what I'd needed.

Soul was glad to have me but didn't make a big deal about it. The idea, as with all spiritual masters, was that I would profit from him infinitely more than he would from me. Was Coyote a spiritual master? Every one of us believed he was, and a wizard as well. It could be that the wizardry disguised or papered over some of his flaws. I've had a long time to think about it in Folsom. What I'm trying to say is that Coyote was either an elevated spirit with fatal flaws, or he was doing devil's work. I know that he wanted to propagate a utopian nation in the desert after his own image. Which is why he encouraged the tribe to make babies and he himself knocked up a bunch of the fems. But like I said, even now, with Jesus inside me, I'm not sure which of the two Soul was, God or Satan.

There is no point in lying about the murder I committed that got me this life sentence. Andy Hassler was a studio musician who made pretty good jack. He was also gay and dug me, sexually speaking. Somehow wacky Roxi had gotten close to Andy, and it was Roxi who told Soul that Andy inherited $25,000 after his father's death. This was when Soul was getting more and more uptight about arming ourselves against the evil empire. Not just the corporate institutions but the humans who worshipped them—they were sheep, lemmings, but they were degraded and themselves evil. That's what Soul was telling us.

After Roxi got into Soul's ear, Soul said that since Andy dug me, it was up to me to cop the $25,000. My first approach, Soul said, would be to soften Andy up by letting him suck my cock. Then pry loose the $$. If that didn't work snuff him. Soul gave me one of the buck knives that were suddenly all over the ranch and told me to go with Roxi.

I didn't like that assignment at all. I didn't understand why we needed so much bread. I didn't want to have sex with Andy Hassler. And most of all I didn't want to kill him.

With Roxi watching, I let Andy suck me off, then tried to get at his money. But he kept denying that he had an inheritance. I hit him several times hard in the face and he still denied it. Finally I phoned Soul and he came over in 20 minutes wearing a short machete-like blade on his belt. Without saying anything, Soul pulled the blade and sliced Andy across the left side of his face, almost severing his ear. Andy crumpled onto the floor, whimpering, blood gushing everywhere.

Soul said to me: "Ask him one more time. If he doesn't give us the bread," Soul motioned to the buck knife strapped to my ankle, "do 'im."

I said, "What if Roxi was wrong? What if he doesn't have the bread?"

Roxi said, "I ain't wrong, Cupid."

Soul said, "I know what he has and what he don't have, bro."

I stabbed Andy in the neck. Stabbed him three times and killed him. Soul and Roxi were in the kitchen. When it was over Soul told Roxi to use a towel to soak up some of Andy's blood and smear a bloody message on the walls. The word Soul came up with was **RIX** and Roxi did what he told her.

At the trial it came out that Andy actually did inherit $25,000, which he ended up protecting with his life.

The police pulled my Camaro over a few days later and found the murder weapon in the glove compartment. Even now I can't tell you why I didn't just chuck the buck knife in the desert someplace. Maybe I felt that my old good luck would continue, even though the signs—if only I could read them—were saying the opposite.

Hedda and some of the other tribe said the murders of Self, Gallo and Hassler would look like copycat. But how? Roxi smeared **RIX** on the walls in Andy's house, and the Self-Gallo murders had **CRO** and **TOX**, which the whole world knew about. How's that supposed to convince the police that those murders and the Hassler murder were committed by the same party, and that I must therefore be innocent and released? Needless to say, the cops didn't buy the copycat deal. They transferred me from the LA County Jail to Soledad, from there to Quentin, and then, six years ago to Folsom, where I am now. Minister Cupid in the sacred heart of Jesus. And not the false Jesus either.

As soon as I was imprisoned in the LA County Jail, a whole lot of fems started writing me letters, and that pretty much has continued until this day. Some of them asked how I escaped the gas chamber. Actually I was given a death sentence and put on death row in Soledad, but then it was commuted to life.

In winter 1970, six black kids were gassed for "wilding" in Golden Gate Park, meaning they got out of control and gang-raped. But then, after their executions, it turned out they were innocent. The female that said she was gang-raped admitted to having lied at the urging of the DA's office. The ACLU sued and while the wilding case was moving up the courts, all pending executions nationwide were postponed. The Supreme Court finally ruled that despite the witness's recantation, the execution of the six black kids *was* legal. And capital punishment was reinstated.

But then, in a weird twist, the Supreme Court said that all of the death row inmates whose executions had been postponed while the courts were deliberating would have their sentences commuted to life imprisonment. So me and others from the tribe and Soul himself, who were all supposed to die, are doing life.

I had prepared myself to die. But I thank Jesus I am still alive. I ended up getting married to one of the females that was emailing me, a good Christian lady. I won't divulge her name.

Then, three years after I established my ministry and two years after my marriage, the prison authorities changed my status to permit monthly conjugal visits.

We have five great kids, four boys and a girl. Matthew, Mark, Luke, and John. The girl we named Cher.

Head Games
(21 years after, Federal Correctional Institution, Alderson, W. Va.)

Just about everyone I come in contact with smells like something.

Soul smelled like rosewood, sweet and clean and fresh, of the earth. All the time I spent with Soul, even in the desert where we couldn't wash regularly, he had that same rosewood smell.

Soul gave everyone tribe names, but it was Roxi who hit on Head Games, which I guess referred to my environmental activism and my attempts to outmaneuver the politicians. I never liked the name because it doesn't fit my sense of who I am. But it stuck.

Soul also called me Green because of my passion for wilderness. He gave color names to most of the tribe who were close to him. Roxi, he called Black because of her dark moods. Mercy was Blue because of the clarity in her thinking. Loca, he called Orange because of her wildness and daring. Lori-Kay Woerman—Worm—Soul called Red because of her sexual energy. Cupid, Soul called Purple because of his flamboyance. Tex Embry was Gray because he was so impressionable.

I grew up in Escondido, just north of San Diego. My father was military and when I was little my family moved from one base to another—Germany, Korea, Saudi Arabia, North Carolina—but I don't remember any of them. By the time I was in school my dad was retired from the service and doing some kind of consulting work for the city, or maybe it was the county. He could have been CIA for all I know. Him and my mom had divorced when I was in fourth grade. Only they both stayed in the northern San Diego area—my dad lived in San Marcos—and he would visit us. I have a younger sister named Lizbeth—we call her Sissie—and an older half-brother, Hunter, that my mom had from a previous marriage.

My mom used to do office work part-time. These days she doesn't do much but watch TV and drink sweet wine.

My high school years were not much different from other American teenagers. I was a cheerleader. In my junior year I was in a modern dance class with nine other girls and four boys, and people liked it so much that we went on tour in San Francisco, San Jose, and Seattle. I dated boys but I was conservative sexually. People who have read or seen the lies on TV about Coyote and his wild tribe girls find this hard to believe, but I was a virgin until I met Soul in San Francisco at the age of eighteen.

In my senior year I took a creative writing class with a gifted teacher named Mr. Van Doren and discovered that I had a talent—a small talent—for writing. He encouraged me to go to college to expand my creative side, and when I was feeling confident—emotionally strong—I considered going on to college. But that wasn't the way I usually felt. I still think of Mr. Van Doren with affection. He had a comforting smell about him, vanilla with an undercurrent of cherry pipe tobacco.

The biggest difference between me and other girls my age was that I was more often than not unhappy, fretful, depressed. But it wasn't so much about myself as what I saw around me—the poisoning of the environment, money madness, cruelty to plants and animals, the me-first mentality.

People who write or—these days—email me here in prison ask about my interest in the environment. It must have started from living in Escondido. When I was real young Escondido was almost like country, with grassy hills and chaparral and large deciduous trees; hundreds of bird species; wild mammals like the coyote, the red and gray fox, the cougar in the higher elevations.

But then the real predator, big business, got into it, clearing the bush to build unnecessary housing and condos, strip malls to service the housing, and needless to say, more and more traffic and pollution. There was not enough water, so it had to be imported from Oregon and Utah, which meant shortages and sometimes foul water to drink. To make space for real estate, the chaparral was broken up and trees and fragile native plants were uprooted, scarring the earth, but none of the important people saw the scars.

They put a so-called non-binding referendum on the ballot on whether they should build a nuclear power plant. It lost by a huge margin, so they went ahead and built it anyhow in the Mesa Grande Indian Reservation, close to where my family lived. The Indians didn't want anything to do with the nuclear plant, but they were poor and it was forced on them.

Why was this tremendous harm done? One word: Profit.

I always loved wilderness and was passionate about protecting it, but I had no organizational skills and didn't know any of the important people. Ironically, it was only when I became notorious as one of Coyote's tribe girls that I had the authority—the clout—to found **ATWA**, which stands for Air, Trees, Water, Animals. **ATWA** means the planting of trees, cleaning up the oil slicks—or, better, preventing them from happening.

ATWA fights the nuclear industry and chemical pollution. It fights the hunters and the fur industry. I have some loyal people outside prison that maintain **ATWA.**

I've been in prison 21 years and I still receive lots of mail from all over the world: Europe, Canada, Australia, Japan, Korea, Israel. But it's only Americans that ask if I was molested by my father, or even insinuate that I must have been, like there is no other reason to be unhappy when you're young. The answer is no. My father and mother divorced, but they were good to me and Sissie, my little sister—or tried to be.

The vast majority of the correspondence I get is less interested in me than in Jesus Coyote, and I understand that. I'm more interested in Jesus Coyote than I am in Hedda Hayman. And if you knew him without the prejudice and spite and hate he's been saddled with by this maddening country and its official media, you might understand why it is ordinary people are so fascinated by him.

You know that I was arrested for attempting to assassinate President Gerald Ford when he came to Sacramento in 1975. Ford wasn't evil but he allowed himself to be manipulated by big business which set about to bulldoze the last remaining wildernesses in our country. And he pardoned that evil warmonger Nixon.

It was a rainy day in Sacramento, and because I'm a small person with red hair and freckles, they let me get close enough to Ford to smell him. It was a neutral smell, almost mineral, which testified to Ford's dullness and lack of empathy. Not a good karmic smell, especially for someone with his power to do harm. But even if he deserved to die that does not mean I intended to kill him.

As was brought out at my trial, the Taurus was loaded but the slide was not pulled back. The gun was not in firing position when I pointed it at him. Why did I point at him in the first place? Anger, rage—but not the senselessness to try to assassinate him.

Maybe there's another reason I got myself arrested, and that is something I didn't say at the trial. I felt guilty being on the outside when Soul and Bitch, Chong, Ho, GJ, Loca, Mercy, and Billy Sans-Soleil were in prison, serving long terms, even life. At first most of them—and Soul of course—were given death, which was then, unexpectedly, commuted because of some legalism.

I said to myself that if these maroons were willing to put their lives on the line for Soul, why not me? If the closest human we have to Jesus reborn is kept in solitary, shackled day and night, why not me?

Now that I'm in Alderson for the rest of my natural life, I feel like I made the right decision. I was never interested in becoming an American mom. I don't miss the sex because I lost all interest in sex after Soul was imprisoned. And being in prison in West Virginia does not mean that I'm further removed from Soul. Authorities never did allow any of Soul's tribe to visit or even talk with him on the phone.

When I broke out of Sybil Brand it was because I heard the rumor about Soul's cancer, that he was dying of testicular cancer. He was my lover and brother and divine teacher, and now they said he was dying. I had to see him.

But somebody I thought I trusted turned me in and they transferred me to CIW—California Institute for Women, in Frontera. After almost two years there they moved me to this federal prison in Alderson, W. Va.

It turned out that Soul didn't have cancer, that it was just another cruel rumor about the Man-God people love to hate.

I pursue my same interests here, in Alderson, that I had outside, mostly environmental issues like I said. **ATWA**. Plus I don't have to worry about supporting myself. It's true that prison food sucks, especially for a vegan, but I was never hung up on eating. There is some animosity from other inmates and from the staff, mostly because they object to my devotion to Soul, but I had the same animosity on the outside.

The Jesus Rainbow Ministry, in Lexington, Kentucky, serves as my official surrogate. I express myself on **ATWA** and other issues and the JR Ministry prints and sends my writings to concerned people all over the country. The Ministry didn't insist that I become a born-again Christian either like some of the tribe did.

That disappointed me, tribe people becoming born-agains. I guess they figured it was their best way of getting paroled or being transferred to a looser prison with conjugal visits. Or maybe they just let themselves forget what all of the tribe once knew, that the true Jesus is alive and shackled in solitary confinement in Pelican Bay Prison. That he needs our support more than ever.

People on the outside have said that if Jesus Coyote was both a God and a magician like his tribe said, why would he allow himself to get arrested and rot away his life out of the world's sight?

Well, you can ask the same question of the historical Jesus. Why did he sacrifice himself where he did, when he did?

Myself, I am not in a position to question Soul's martyrdom. It just hurts to see him suffer so.

Something else I spend time on here in Alderson is embroidering Soul's vest. The tribe girls began working on the vest many years ago in the movie ranch, weaving in strands of our hair, stitching in animal and desert plant figures, because Soul is so good with animals and growing things. The vest is jade green corduroy, with embroidered leather patches, old silver coins a Death Valley prospector gave us, strands of hair from many of the tribe girls, and natural figures—animals, plants, mountains—in multi-colored threads.

We started embroidering when those Hollywood murders happened and everything went haywire. The vest was then confiscated by LASO for no good reason since Soul was already in prison. Finally—I had been in prison for six years—my lawyer, a nice pro bono man who actually smells like my favorite teacher in high school, Mr. Van Doren, managed to get the vest back from LASO before they put it up for auction. Since then I've been working on it almost daily. One of these days I will complete it. But then how will I get it to Soul in Pelican Bay? And will they even let him have it?

I referred to the Hollywood murders, so you want to know my feelings about them. I feel very sorry for the victims, like I would for anyone who suffered violent death. And for the actress with the infant in her belly I feel particularly sorry. But I am still not convinced that the actual murderers have been arrested. Remember the pair of wraparound mirror shades that were found at the scene. Those shades didn't belong to any of the victims or to any of the tribe that was arrested. So who did they belong to?

Anyway, why are those Hollywood deaths worse than the minute-to-minute death of our invisible homeless people, or worse than the genociding of our wilderness?

Soul is in solitary wearing shackles because he was supposed to have masterminded those murders. But that's a lie. The murderous violence is everywhere around us. The American government is committed to murder.

Soul used to say that he was dead in the head. He meant that he simply reflected what those around him thought. And everywhere the thinking was and is violence. That's why we kept moving farther and farther into Death Valley. To get away from the mindless violence. Only you can't get away from it.

Some people have claimed that the government manipulated the Hollywood murders to set up a mock trial that would put the tribe and so-called counter-culture in a bad light, dupe the public into believing idealistic young people were criminals, even terrorists. And transform a God into a devil by exploiting Jesus Coyote as the fall guy.

I can believe it. Doing what we did, moving into the outback, fending for ourselves, made it much harder for them to manipulate our bodies and minds, turn us into good little 8:00 to 6:00 clones who stare at the monitor in our cubicle, eat cheeseburgers and vote Republican or Democrat. More and more young people were refusing to buy that, which infuriated authority. When they got wind that Soul was having great success in attracting these same young people and constructing a counter-nation based on utopian principles, they decided to erase the maroons.

Maroon is a word Soul came up with that derives from escaped slaves in the Caribbean who became revolutionaries not because they welcomed bloodshed but because they wanted to live decent, peaceful lives.

I met Soul when I was visiting a cousin in San Francisco. I was sitting on a bench in Golden Gate Park when he sat down next to me. He didn't have his beard then but he had those eyes of course. And he had that sweet, clean, earthy rosewood smell. I remember he was wearing a small cap, like a skullcap or a fez. But the stranger thing was that he wore a harmonica around his neck, like what Bob Dylan used to wear so that he could blow into the harmonica while strumming his guitar.

Soul said to me: "You're sad."

I nodded, since I was looking at the dog litter and the used condom litter and the untended trees and bushes, hearing the honking traffic and thinking about how crapped up the environment was and how little people seemed to care.

He said: "I'm a gardener."

Then he said: "I tend to the flower children of the Haight. I plant seeds and see that the children grow straight and lush."

I picked my head up and looked at him.

He said: "You're a flower child and I can see you need tending."

"How can you see that?"

"Your eyes. And how you clench your fists. What's your name?"

"Hedda."

"Listen to this song, pretty Hedda:

Don't cry for what's past, little flower,
Don't fret for tomorrow,
Minute by minute is forever,
Be here now, fragrant flower.
Be here now.

He blew sweet sad chords on his harmonica, then looked at me, his beautiful dark eyes filled with light, that rosewood scent all about him.

He said: "Do you want to go with me, pretty Hedda?"

"Where?"

"Who knows," he said. "I don't punch a time clock, and I ain't never gonna. You see, pretty Hedda, I been in prison where there's not a minute that's your own. I don't plan on ever goin' back. Does that scare you?"

"What?"

"Me being in prison."

"Why were you there? What did you do?"

"What I done was get myself born poor."

I understood just what he meant. And I went with him. I phoned my sister who I was very close with and said I wouldn't be coming home for a while. Sissie started crying. I told her that I met a wonderful being, that I would be in touch with her and sometime fairly soon I would come back for her.

I was 18-years-old and I went with Soul. I was the second girl in the tribe after Mercy. At that time there were a lot of cool young people in the Haight, which is where we crashed. Soul showed me love and he showed me fuck. Dickerson, the deputy DA that prosecuted the case, then wrote that lying book, made a big deal about Soul saying he was the God of fuck. It was me he said it to. Somebody had given him a car, an old Chevy convertible—people were always giving him gifts—and the three of us, Soul, Mercy and me, were driving north. We were all in the front, Soul driving, me between him and Mercy. The top was down, the sun was bright, the air smelled like fresh berries. We were singing songs and harmonizing.

Soul knew I was a virgin and he told me to say "fuck." I wasn't used to swearing and couldn't do it. He said it again: "Say fuck." I still couldn't do it.

"It's only a word," he said. "You shouldn't be afraid of a word just because people that are afraid of their own bodies tell you it isn't right or isn't clean.

Say fuck, little flower."

So I said it. "Fuck."

"I am the God of fuck," he said. Then he pulled over into a grove of Redwoods, spread a blanket on the grass and fucked me on the grass under the wide blue sky, in the godly shadow of the Redwoods. I bled into the earth of the Redwoods. I smelled the salt blood of my womb being absorbed by the spicy sweet moist earth.

Mercy watched with a little unjealous smile on her face.

Then he fucked Mercy while I watched.

Then we got back into the car and continued the drive. And I said to myself without sound: He is the *God of fuck.*

Just then Soul looked at me and said, "What are you smiling at, pretty Hedda?"

I just shrugged my shoulders and kept smiling.

I was pretty, I guess, and people told me that I had a voluptuous figure. But I never thought of myself as being a sexual person. Until Soul. When he touched my body with his hands and tongue and cock, it was as if I was never touched before.

Every girl he fucked, which means every girl that passed through the tribe, even the sexually experienced girls, felt the same way. Roxi, who became the third girl in the tribe, was very experienced and cynical about the possibility of real sexual tenderness—sexual healing like Marvin Gaye would say—but Soul got to Roxi. They fucked just once and she dropped everything to join the tribe.

Roxi is someone that had a peculiar smell. It was sweet but at the same time sharp, acrid, like apples turning to vinegar. It was not a good karmic smell really. It was like her sweetness and naturalness had been twisted by the shitty violent life she was forced to live. Roxi was just 18, like me, when she met Soul, but she'd already been through the mill: prostitution, prison, some kind of devil worship business in San Francisco. She'd lived on the streets. With all that she was beautiful and sexy, only with that bad karmic smell. But after being in the tribe for just a little while, being next to Soul, her smell became sweet and fresh again, the way it must've been when she was very young. It was her own natural smell that Soul gifted her with.

I haven't seen Roxi in more than 20 years, but I'd guess that her smell has become sharp and acrid again since she turned on Soul and the tribe.

People scoff when followers call Soul the modern-day Jesus, scorned and despised by the authorities and money-maniacs in the same way the first Jesus was. But we who were close to him know what he is. Like Jesus, Soul talked in parables, not for effect, but because parables were a vivid, forceful way of making his teaching understood.

Soul made a point of always stopping for hitchhikers. And on that same trip, with Mercy and me, driving up north on the ocean highway, near Eureka, Soul picked up a hitchhiker, a broken-down older man who looked like he hadn't slept under a roof in a long time. He carried an old overstuffed briefcase which probably contained all his possessions. He climbed into the car and sat in the back real quiet.

We were driving when Soul said out of the blue: "What if I trade you all the money in my pockets for all the money in yours?"

The hobo was like, "What?"

Soul repeated: "I'll give you every cent I have in my pockets if you give me every cent you have in yours."

The hobo seemed to think it over, but then said, "No, I don't think so."

"You sure?" Soul said.

"Yeah, I'm sure."

Soul persisted. "Here I am driving a convertible car with two beautiful young ladies. And there you were on the highway with a rusted old briefcase containing everything you've got in the world. But still I'm willing to swap you every penny I have in my pockets for whatever you're carrying in your pockets. Think about it. You want to swap?"

"No, no, I don't think so."

"Show me how much money you have on you," Soul said.

After hesitating, the hobo dug through his pockets and came up with a few crumpled dollar bills, some dimes, nickels, pennies.

"That it?" Soul said.

"Uh-huh."

"Lookit what all I have," Soul said, pulling out a fat roll of twenties and a smaller roll of fifties. "I have two thousand dollars right here."

The hobo was amazed. "You mean you were ready to give all that money to me?"

"That's right. If you weren't so hung up on the few dollars you were carrying you would've been carrying a couple thousand. Man, don't be hung up on money. Let it go and it will take care of itself. But only if you really let it go, hear."*

Crescent City is a rainy, wooded, working-class city in Del Norte county, CA, near the Oregon border. It is also where Pelican Bay State Prison is at, though the prison is hard to find because there are no signs leading to it.

We stopped in Crescent City and stayed in a motel. I still remember the name, Rain Dance. The Rain Dance Motel. We pushed the two motel twin beds together and slept all three in the same bed. And this time we didn't just watch while Soul made love to one of us. We made love all together, and it was very sweet. It was one of the things that Soul impressed on everyone in the tribe, that we can experience physical joy from a person of the same sex, even from a child, if the child is treated with gentleness. In America there is a paranoia about child molestation, but that's because the body is seen as private property, another kind of capital. With us the body was communal property, and children's feelings were respected not condescended to.

The next morning Soul offered us another lesson. He called Mercy and me into the bathroom while he was on the toilet and motioned us to sit down on the tile. We sat there on the floor by his feet while he groaned and grunted in a loud, exaggerated, even comical way. It was—to us—shocking, but also funny. We watched and heard and smelled him shit and wipe and flush, then the three of us left the bathroom holding hands. It was just another of Soul's simple lessons in divesting ourself of culture's artificialness and submitting to our human nature, which is also our animal and spiritual nature.**

On the way back to San Francisco, Soul picked up another hitchhiker and it was LuAnn Hoy, who had run away from her home in New Jersey. Soul made love to her in the back of the convertible while Mercy drove, and so Ho, which is what we called LuAnn, was initiated into the tribe. Back in the Haight, Loca—Daria Luz Shriver—joined up with us. And Bruce Keith also joined, just the second male, after Soul. Bruce Keith was in his early thirties maybe, short, broad-shouldered, with an intense, serious face and a stubble beard. We called him Sarge. He rolled his own cigarettes and didn't talk a whole lot. We didn't know much about him besides that he served hard time in Soledad for a violent crime of some kind. Sarge was real good with his hands, anything mechanical. He had a very male smell, like motor oil.

After ten days or so in the Haight, Soul said let's split. Only we were nine now and needed something larger than the Chevy convertible. As usual at that time, providence intervened and Soul charmed some eccentric rich human from Marin County into trading us his big school bus for the convertible. Since we weren't legally able to drive a yellow school bus we painted it black and outfitted it with beds, rugs, cushions, a refrigerator. We called it Scorpion.

The scorpion was one of Soul's totem animals, along with the coyote and rattler.

By the time we left the Haight in our Scorpion, Mooch—Mary-Jeanne Butterfield—and Lamar Cady, who we called Fang, had also joined up with us. Mooch came from a wealthy family in Santa Fe and had been a debutante and all that. But then someone turned her onto acid and when she came down she was a different human with different values. She had a good wit and airy disposition. She smelled like cold, fresh chocolate milk.

Fang was another story, a burly tattooed biker with the Skull Helmets. He had protruding teeth on top which is the reason for his nickname. He was also maybe slightly retarded. But he was good-natured, seemingly devoted to Soul, and like Sarge he was a great mechanic, so when the bus or anything else broke down, between Fang and Sarge it would always get fixed. Fang had long red hair which he didn't wash, which is what he smelled of: unwashed hair.

Fang and Sarge shared the driving with Soul, but it was Soul who drove the bus up and around the cliffs north of San Francisco into Oregon. Then Sarge took over and drove east to Idaho, down into Wyoming and Utah. We always felt the incongruity between the vast, beautiful wilderness or semi-wilderness, and the tiny-souled humans that worked and lived and ruled in these places. It was those small robotic souls, on behalf of their "parent" institutions, that were responsible for despoiling the natural environment.

We were still picking up people. When we'd camp for the night, Soul would make sure we all made love with every new maroon, girl or boy. You can call them orgies, if you like. For us they were love-fests.

There have been rumors that our love-fests were filmed, and people who write to me often ask me about that. Why would that matter so much? Actually, I know the answer. It's sex in the head. Which is a dangerous place for sex to be, especially in this culture.

Yes, Sarge often filmed us, and when he was involved in the loving, someone else would film. No, I don't know where the prints of those movies are. Probably someone has made or is planning to make a lot of money out of them the way they've made money out of Soul and the tribe. I can't even count how many books and articles and movies and so-called documentaries have been made about us, without even knowing or wanting to know who and what we really were.

People who write me ask about dope. Of course there was dope: grass, hash, mushroom, ecstasy, acid. Except for a rare toke on a joint, I'd never used dope until I met Soul. When I became familiar with the various substances, I preferred the natural highs like mushroom and peyote and hash. But Soul's philosophy was that we use the technology that people idolized against itself. So we did chemical dope like ecstasy, mescaline, and acid to extend and affirm life, in opposition to the chemical technology that was devoted to compressing life while accumulating profit.

Soul knew someone in the Santa Susana Mountains who'd offered him space on a ranch in exchange for work. That was the Harker movie ranch where the tribe lived off and on for all the time we were in that area, sometimes squatting both there and in Death Valley.

It was soon after we arrived in LA that Billy Sans-Soleil showed up one day at the movie ranch with his three girlfriends. Billy was cool, handsome with boyish features and a soft fuzzy beard. He was like a pretty bad boy, which made him real popular with the girls. We called him Cupid. He smelled faintly of lime, fresh and natural and alive. Which is how he was pretty much all the time, even when he was tripping. Though he was young, just 20, he'd already done time in Quentin, I think it was. Sixteen or eighteen months for assaulting his father who had been molesting him.

Cupid also acted in porn and legit movies, and he'd been involved for a brief time in devil worship. That wasn't unusual for maroons who were searching for some alternative to the shitty mainstream and sometimes took odd turns before they hit on the real thing. Cupid had a relaxed, confident manner and him and Soul hit it off right away.

Those few years of living, loving, sharing, working and being close to Soul in the desert and on the ranch were the happiest days of my life.

Some people have commented on the so-called encounter sessions based on fear that Soul organized. Soul knew a lot of ways to get humans to confront themselves and each other, including psychological-type games he'd picked up from his years in prison and from his wide reading, and—more than anything—from his intuition.

Using the coyote as an example, Soul conveyed to us that a life well lived was based on an awareness of our fear. This was not paranoia but the grim reality that the dominant culture foisted on us. It was only by understanding fear and where it came from that we could be free. Or as free as we could possibly be given our brief lifespan and the finiteness of our messed-over planet.

You want to know my opinion of the former tribe members who copped a plea and turned on Soul to save their own skin. I'll leave out Fang—Lamar Cady—because he just got drunk and shot his mouth. But the others—Li'l Bess, Donkey Don, Roxi—I think they're Judases. Plus their betrayal hasn't done them much good. Roxi and Donkey Don are still inside; Donkey Don was attacked by inmates in Soledad and almost killed. He lost one eye and partial sight in the other. Li'l Bess—Elizabeth Ginzburg—aborted her baby which was her baby by Soul. Then she lost both of her rich parents in a plane crash. Since then she's been busted for drugs several times and badly beaten up in the LA County Jail. So I guess you can say that their karma is paying them back in spades.

Night of the Thousand Knives

Joya Grove, 8 Aug '69

Billy Strayhorn

I met Tim Holt for the first time last night at the Hell Posse concert.

My friend Bruno had to leave, and Timmy was alone, so afterward him and I shared a joint and went to Degrade, the java joint on the Boulevard.

Turned out we had a lot in common.

We both liked the same bands—the freaky metal ones.

In fact both of us had the same Hell Posse tat—a bleeding heart punctured by a knife with a grinning death's head on the hilt.

It was supposed to be inspired by Tantra.

That's Tibetan.

I had the tat on my butt, Timmy had his on his left calf.

Both of us were the same age, 19, and were even born in the same month, me July 12, Timmy July 19.

We both wore Rasta dreads.

We both dug Orange Sunshine and Thai stick.

Timmy invited me over to this property he was caretaking in the Hills.

He told me Naomi Self was living in the main house with some other rich movie people.

I dug Naomi in *Vampire Daughters in Beverly Hills.*

I liked *Revulsion* too, which her husband made, the Polish director, Hora.

You can say I'm into the freaky side of things.

But I'm also a totally average guy that does average things like go to college (I'm an Accounting major), watch sports on TV, get high.

I like sex too—pretty much any way I can get it.

That night me and Timmy went to a late movie in Glendale, then went back to his place.

The movie was Jaroslav Hora's *Night of the Thousand Knives.*

I dug it okay, but I kept getting these weird flashes.

It's hard to explain.

Like I was seeing figures behind the figures, very faint, always in motion.

It could have been the lines we snorted in the bathroom before the movie started.

Or maybe I was seeing my death.

The terrible way I was murdered.

For no reason. I didn't deserve to die. I was just 19.

The movie let out about 12:30 and we went back to Tim's in two cars.

We hung out in his apartment, smoked some Thai, listened to music.

When I left Tim's it was about 3:15 a.m.

I was in my Karmann Ghia cutting across the property to get back on the street, when someone stepped out of the darkness and motioned me to stop.

I shouldn'ta stopped but I did.

I opened the window and was about to explain I was just visiting the caretaker, when he pulled open the door and without a word started stabbing.

Him and the girls all had knives.

He was tall, bony, older than me, but not by much.

I watched his eyes as he was stabbing me.

Stab after stab. I wondered why he didn't stop. I was already dead.

He wasn't even looking at me.

He was looking through me.

I saw myself in his eyes, light blue like mine.

He wore a hooded sweatshirt—purple or navy blue—over his head, but I could see he had long blond hair and a blond walrus mustache.

He wore torn jeans and was barefoot.

Which was weird. What's he doing barefoot in this part of town?

As he was stabbing me with that hammering-hammering, everything slowed down and I thought: Maybe he's homeless.

But I could see he wasn't homeless.

There were three girls, young, slim, wearing black or dark-colored minis, barefoot, carrying knives, not saying a word.

They were watching him kill me, blood spurting all over the inside of the car.

I was there in the metallic green Karmann Ghia watching them watch him stab me, like on a screen.

Then the screen became the movie I just saw with Tim: *Night of the Thousand Knives.*

Behind the scenes in the movie was another movie, harder to see, dimmer.

Now I saw that the dim movie behind the movie was him stabbing me and them watching in that way.

The movie behind the movie moved fast, maybe twice the speed of how it really was.

I don't understand why it was so speeded up.

I remember not screaming. It happened so fast.

But the other reason was somehow I expected it.

Getting murdered.

I can't explain.

It had to do with the silent movie behind the movie.

When I left Timmy he was sitting on the floor, leaning against the wall.

He was asleep, with an open bottle of Corona in his fist.

His mouth was twisted in a weird way.

Tim's parents live in Pasadena, and so does my mom.

My dad died in a car crash when I was 14.

I think I will be seeing him.

My mom never remarried.

Tim said his dad was a forensic pathologist.

Worked with corpses.

Cadavers.

What's the difference between a corpse and a cadaver?

I remember that Tim's dad's name was Rodney. Rod.

My dad's name was Ruud, which is Dutch.

He immigrated to the US from the Netherlands when he was real young.

He was a radiologist.

He was killed in a car crash in Malta where he was supposed to deliver a lecture.

I have no idea how it would be to live in Malta.

I'm not sure where Malta is, though I remember my dad showing it to us on the map.

Could be that's where you go when you die—Malta.

Cadaver is when the corpse is dissected. Cut into.

Like what they'll do to me.

Count and measure the wounds.

Determine why.

Why I was murdered that way.

I didn't know anyone.

I wasn't doing anything except leaving a friend's place.

Sure, we got high…

Like I said, I didn't scream. There was no talk.

There were sounds. Each hard stab or thrust made a deep sharp sound.

Like a wild guitar riff. Belladonna, lead guitar of Toxic.

Heeeow! Heeeow! Heeeeeow!

Something else: The killer looked like someone.

The tall bony killer in the purple hooded sweatshirt.

Torn jeans. Barefoot, silent.

Hammering.

I was dying when I thought: why don't the girls stab too?

They're watching without any expression on their faces.

Maybe they're getting off on it.

I saw Belladonna once in a bar in Hollywood.

He was with Celine, his girlfriend. Lover.

Belladonna, leaning against the bar, was wearing soft black leather pants, very tight, Jim Morrison style.

I could see his cock snaking down his thigh.

I can't remember if it was his left or right thigh.

Celine was all in purple, with her thick wavy red hair trailing down her back.

I remember now.

The tall bony killer with the purple hooded sweatshirt stabbing me, stabbing, looks like my father.

Dad in Malta.

Dead.

Kristin Barrett

Phillip Morris heiress, that's who I am.

Kristin Barrett the Phillip Morris heiress.

Is that better than being the Trojan Condom heiress? Or the Charmin Toilet Paper heiress?

Please remember that I majored in Comparative Literature at Smith College, that institution of privilege.

Home to Sylvia Plath, who also died young.

She died, though, by her own hand.

In her tormented way, she chose how she wanted to die.

I didn't want to die this way, stabbed and stabbed by crazed intruders.

What could they want?

I never thought I made enough of an impression to offend anyone.

Unless it was my "fortune" that offended them, on principle.

I don't think so. None of them muttered anything about *class* or *money.*

Maybe it was my affiliation with Viktor and his affiliation with Jaroslav Hora that provoked them.

Jaro made shocking films.

But many directors make shocking films, and much more crudely, without Jaro's refinement.

These killers didn't seem the shockable sort.

Maybe it had to do with the beautiful sex-goddess Naomi Self.

But Naomi was as friendly and unpretentious as a schoolgirl.

She won over anyone who met her.

It could have been a symbolic thing, what they—the killers—felt Naomi Self represented.

Don Fernando?

Don Fernando mingled with American royalty: Hollywood movie stars.

He made them look even more beautiful.

And he was a charmer.

True, Don Fernando played around with kinky sex, but that's all it was, playing around.

In LA "vanilla" S/M doesn't even evoke a yawn.

Viktor Hus? My unlikely lover?

Viktor was a Jew, and he had what he jokingly described as a checkered past in Czechoslovakia and Eastern Europe.

Parts of Central and Eastern Europe are considered "lawless" and it is possible that Viktor, who is a kind of impresario, might have made enemies.

But how likely is it that those enemies would wait until he was settled in the US for nine or ten years before deciding to murder him?

Viktor was a playboy whom I managed to harness.

How I managed to harness him is the elusive question.

Plain Jane like me, it couldn't be my looks.

Yes, I was wealthy, but Viktor was quite comfortably off without my money.

He was living the easy life long before I somehow spun into his orbit.

He said he liked all of me, especially my "heart."

By that, he meant my good intentions.

Noblesse Oblige.

I did some work in the so-called inner cities.

I helped establish a foundation for under-privileged girls in the Watts area of LA.

My mother and I did similar work in New Haven.

New Haven isn't just Yale University.

Poor, deprived neighborhoods surround the Yale University complex.

I almost said corporation. Yale University Corporation.

In fact, I was scheduled to fly to Connecticut the next day, 9 August, to dedicate a home for parentless girls in New Haven.

My mother, Eunice Barrett, must be waiting for me at the airport.

Or has she heard that her only daughter Kristin was senselessly murdered, stabbed forty, fifty times for no reason that she could possibly surmise?

I was in the east wing, reading in bed with my granny glasses on my nose, when I saw a slim girl in black with glazed eyes pass by the bedroom.

I smiled and waved to her without thinking to ask what she was doing in our house.

Maybe it was the MDMA tab that Viktor had given me a few hours earlier.

MDMA promotes loving, and how can that be bad?

I was reading a new translation of Kafka's *Amerika.*

After reading this translation, Jaro was so impressed he considered turning it into a film.

That's what I was reading.

Kafka, Jaro and Viktor are all Czech Jews.

In Kafka, the most extraordinary disturbances are recorded as if they were commonplace.

Maybe I was under the dual influences of MDMA and Kafka when I waved and smiled to my executioner.

She returned, this time waving a knife, and ordered me into the living room.

I got out of bed in my nightgown and, barefoot, moved into the living room.

She, the slender executioner, with the glazed look in her eyes, was also barefoot.

She had long, dark brown hair, small even features, wore a black suede miniskirt and had long, shapely legs.

There was something unpleasant about the way she held her mouth.

I let her lead me into the living room without a word of protest.

Naomi, Don Fernando and Viktor were already there.

So were the other executioners: the one in charge: a tall man with a purple hooded sweatshirt, and two other slim young girls in black minis.

They were all barefoot and they all had knives.

I was thinking how unlikely, how utterly absurd it all was.

And I still wasn't frightened.

I remembered that sweet-hearted Naomi had found a lost kitten in the garden and taken it in.

So as not to harm the kitten, she penned her two Doberman guard dogs,

Bod and Soul.

That's what she had named them. Bod was unusually muscular while Soul was shy.

But when guarding they were both aggressive.

The night we were murdered Bod and Soul weren't even on the property.

Thankfully, nothing happened to the kitten which kept out of sight.

I hope someone has the sense to adopt it.

Suddenly the male executioner, who had been silent, loudly ordered Naomi to sit on the floor.

Don Fernando moved forward to protest that Naomi was very pregnant and sitting on the floor was difficult for her.

Without saying a word, the executioner stabbed Don Fernando in the throat.

Then he stabbed him again in the chest.

As Don Fernando toppled to the floor, Viktor grabbed the girl who was guarding him and wrestled her to the floor.

Then he bolted and ran outside.

The others pursued him leaving me with Naomi in the large room.

Naomi was on her knees with her face against the wall.

I wanted to go to her, comfort her.

I couldn't move. As in a terrible dream, I felt rooted to the floor.

Then the first girl with the long dark hair came back and without a word or sign began to stab me.

Somehow, I broke away from her and ran outside into the garden.

I could sense without hearing it that Viktor was being murdered.

The girl executioner caught up with me, and another girl with a knife was now grabbing my shoulder.

I fell to one knee and looked up at both young impassive faces: the one with the long dark hair, regular features and twisted mouth.

The other with long blonde hair and freckles.

They were silent. Their eyes were flat and blank.

I said just one thing:

Take me.

Don Fernando

Everyone knows Brando, obviously.

Marlon was my most famous client and probably my best friend among my clients, until he went bald.

I don't do hair pieces or weaves, so I lost him.

My most famous client now would probably be either Jack Palance or Sal Mineo.

Sorry, I can't tell you if either is gay.

I can but I won't.

A hairdresser is like a lawyer or psychiatrist.

Whatever passes between a client and me is confidential.

So don't ask and I won't tell.

Until I write my tell-all book for a seven-figure advance on royalties.

Just kidding.

Gregory Peck, for the record, has great hair.

Graying of course, but thick and healthy—for his age.

Thanks to me.

But when he's in my chair, hair is not what we talk about.

Hairdressing—especially the way I do it—is intimate.

You say things you simply would not say in another context.

Unless, say, two people were tripping on acid or mescaline.

Now I've done hair after snorting a line, but never after smoking hash or weed.

Coke doesn't affect precision like cannabis does.

When you're getting paid fifteen hundred dollars for an hour and a half's work, you damn well better make sure you're 100 percent in control.

Doing hair under the influence of MDMA might be a kick, especially with a cool client like Jack Nicholson, who I don't do anymore.

From the way he looks at those Lakers games, I think Jack may be doing his own hair.

Big mistake!

Jack, if you're reading this: Come back to Papa.

Don Fernando will restore those good looks you had in *Easy Rider*.

Because of the stigma of my profession, people assume I'm gay.

I'm anything but, okay?

The movie *Shampoo* that Rob Towne and Warren Beatty wrote and Warren starred in was based on the sexcapades of Don Fernando.

Even if it didn't say so in the credits.

They gave me $175,000 for the rights.

Wait a minute.

Shampoo came out in '75 and I was brutally murdered in '69.

I tend to work on male hair, but I have and have had famous female clients.

Faye Dunaway, Deborah Kerr, Katherine Hepburn, Julie Christie…

Very famous, very difficult female clients.

Naomi Self was my client. That's how we met.

Naomi has great hair.

I've got news for you: Naomi has great everything.

Those two and a half years we were together were fun years.

In every way. As lovers, as friends…

Then came Jaroslav.

Like other sensitive women, Naomi has a weakness for artistic genius.

Which is what she thought Jaroslav had.

Of course, Jaroslav presented himself as though he was the sole possessor of artistic genius.

I won't argue the point.

After my initial disappointment, I decided that even if I wasn't a fan of Jaroslav, I loved Naomi so much that I would support her no matter what she did.

Which is why I'm here, 8 Aug '69, in the Joya Grove house, in a burgundy tank top and ivory Calvin jockeys (bikini model) sitting on the edge of Naomi's bed, talking and joking.

Naomi, reclining on her back on the canopied kingsize fourposter, is wearing a translucent tea rose tunic, no bra, mini-panties.

Ensemble by Yves St. Laurent.

Naomi is eight months pregnant.

Pregnancy doesn't agree with some women.

It agrees with Naomi. She looks lustrous. Radiant.

Tonight I rode my Harley.

I wore a cadet blue Gucci leather jerkin, Calvin blue jeans with gold leather accents and coal-black engineer boots from Mr. S, out of San Francisco.

Naomi and I always were naked or next to naked when we lived together, and somehow we never got out of the custom.

My jeans and jacket were neatly folded on the taupe leather wingchair in the corner of Naomi's (and Jaroslav's) bedroom.

I had just snorted a line, and we were laughing together.

Naomi joked that Jaroslav thought they were naming their baby Che after the famous Cuban revolutionary, one of Jaroslav's heroes.

What she secretly had in mind was the last syllable in the name of her favorite designer: Versa**ce**.

Just then a silhouette came into the room, waving something.

A slim brunette, barefoot and dirty-looking, in a black vinyl mini.

In a vague way, I wondered: How did she get into the house?

She was waving a knife.

She ordered us out of bed into the living room.

In the back of my mind someplace I thought: try to disarm her.

But I was afraid that pregnant Naomi would get hurt.

That was a fatal mistake.

No, my fatal mistake was being in the house to begin with.

It occurred to me that I didn't hear the dogs.

Where were Bod and Soul, Naomi's Dobermans?

They should have been guarding outside.

The other three intruders were in the living room with Viktor.

They were all barefoot, unkempt, waving knives.

A tall, gangly young male with a blond handlebar mustache, in a magenta hooded sweatshirt.

Two females in black cotton minis.

One, freckly, with stringy blonde hair; the other with prominent cheekbones, an aquiline nose, and unwashed red hair tied back in a ponytail.

Suddenly Viktor knocked the girl who was guarding him to the floor and ran into the garden.

The two girls ran after him.

I could hear them scuffling outside.

Then I heard sirens and my spirits briefly lifted.

It wasn't sirens.

It must have been the canyons—they play tricks with sound.

Naomi, next to me, was whimpering softly.

The male killer said to her in a loud, disagreeable voice: Shut the fuck up and sit down on the floor.

I moved toward him: "Can't you see she's pregnant?"

He stabbed me in the left shoulder.

When I fell to the carpet on one knee he stabbed me in the upper chest. Then in the throat.

My blood was gushing like an artesian well.

He kept stabbing.

Viktor Hus

My landsman Jaro would joke that he made me.

Meaning that he set me up in LA and Hollywood with so-called influential people.

Jaro didn't make me.

I met and romanced Kristin Barrett the Phillip Morris heiress without Jaro's intercession.

It wasn't Jaro who blessed me with a nine-and-half-inch penis.

Jaro didn't help me establish my six figure "courier" business.

Being born a Czech Jew is, generally speaking, not as difficult as being a Polish Jew or a German Jew.

Not as difficult as being a Gypsy or a dark-skinned Muslim living in Central or Eastern Europe.

But it is far from easy, and large as I am, I had to learn early to maneuver:

Squeeze through hoops and narrow openings.

Make myself plastic and flexible.

Bend forwards and backwards.

Sideways too, if it came to that.

Feign reverence for the official cruelty that dominates and will always dominate.

I never pretended to be a hero or resister.

As I see it, the two conflicting philosophies in the world I inhabit are Promethean and Dionysian.

I chose the second, without apology.

I'm among that small minority of Central European Jews who opted not to worry, beat my breast, cultivate torment.

Actually, Jaro was another Jew devoted to his own pleasures.

Which is why we got along well.

Jaro is miniature, Viktor, kingsize.

Jaro is intense, artistically gifted.

Viktor is a lazy easy-going sod.

Jaro loves women and so does his landsman.

Viktor always lived by his wits and trusted providence.

Then why did it end so soon, so bloodily?

So banally?

Most people live dissatisfied lives and die that way.

A privileged few live charmed lives right to the end.

The most unfortunate are those, like me, for whom everything goes swimmingly, then in an instant you plummet through a trapdoor into the deepest regions of hell.

If every African American feels slavery in his bones, then every Central European Jew feels *pogrom* in his bones.

But these skinny, longhaired intruders were not Cossacks or Nazis.

8 August 1969 was not Germany 1938. *Kristallnacht.*

What was it? What did they want?

My MDMA business was conducted directly with the Dutch.

We were on good terms.

Even had we not been, these dirty American longhairs would not be the Dutch's assassins of choice.

Like Germans, the Dutch are precise and efficient in matters of killing.

In other ways, they are of course very different from the Germans.

What the longhair intruders actually wanted of us was one question.

The other question was: How did three barefoot girls in miniskirts and their skinny barefoot *capo* overpower us?

Or overpower Don Fernando and me, since Naomi and even Kristin were not in position to fight back.

An hour and a half before I had swallowed 125 milligrams of pure MDMA.

I gave Kristin half a dose because she was especially responsive to the drug. She was scheduled to fly the next morning to the East Coast, and I didn't want the MDMA to disturb her sleep.

The 125 milligrams I swallowed transformed real into surreal, while retarding my reflexes.

Was the skinny long-hair invasion real?

It slaughtered me.

It slaughtered all of us.

Still I didn't believe it was happening, and even now, dead, I can't quite believe it.

Could it be that I was never really alive to begin with?

Or not alive in the sense that I imagined?

Maybe I, and all of us in the Joya Grove house, were imagined—or programmed—by some more elevated entity who simply grew tired of us.

Ceci n'est pas une knife.

When the male stabbed Don Fernando and I saw the spurting blood, I knew the knife *was* real.

I yanked the blonde-haired girl to the floor by her hair and ran outside.

But the MDMA was disorienting and they caught up with me.

I slapped one of the other girls and pulled *her* hair, but then the *capo*, the ringleader, was there, stabbing me with his knife.

Then all four of them were stabbing me, blow after blow after blow.

Still, I managed to get up from the ground, and with my blood spurting and dripping like red, red wine at a *Walpurgisnacht*, I ran farther into the garden.

Again they caught up and resumed killing me.

Knife blows all over my body.

I remember looking up at their faces from the grass, wet and slimy with blood.

They wore weird white Phantom of the Opera masks.

All four of them, stabbing me in turn, rhythmically.

But silently, none of them made a sound.

The single thing I heard was my blood coursing.

Naomi Self

I named the abandoned ebony kitty Roxi.

Roxi was my name in *Vampire Daughters in Beverly Hills,* which is how I met Jaro.

Roxi must have been hiding while they were murdering us.

I thank God for that at least.

I still can't believe that sweet kitty could bring us all such bad luck.

If I didn't find her—if she didn't find me—Bod and Soul would have guarded the property and kept the murderers out.

At least they would have warned us so that we could call the police.

Mother liked Jaro but my father had his doubts.

Dad was put off by Jaro's attraction to blood and gore and demonism.

I tried to explain that Jaro's filmic ideas were a part of his creative personality.

Not at all how he was away from filming.

Dad was polite but unconvinced.

My dad is a Colonel in the Special Forces.

West Point graduate.

It is hard for him not to think like a soldier.

He loved me and wanted the best for me.

Because he loved me he ended up accepting my love for Jaro.

He was elated when I became pregnant with Che.

No, it isn't a name my dad would have chosen.

My baby dead, slaughtered.

I worry for them all after the murders.

My father, mother, my sister Nara.

We all loved each other so much.

They were all so happy about my baby.

Poor Jaro. Our time together was short.

Why didn't they kill me but not kill my baby?

So close to being born.

I felt him every day and night and whispered and sang to him.

Jaro and I thought the counter-culture kids were cool.

Relaxed, sexy, bucking the tide.

And I liked the look: tie-dye, buckskin, bare feet, no makeup, no bras.

And here they are stabbing, slaughtering us.

I don't understand.

It must have to do with me.

And maybe Jaro.

The films we made together.

The way Jaro and I were portrayed in the media: freaky, beautiful people with our special coterie of joy seekers.

That isn't the way we were.

Jaro is an artistic genius with a unique vision.

But he himself is not freaky. Neither am I.

I know people find me physically appealing, but that aside, I'm totally normal.

It's true of course that I'm an actress.

But my plans were not to act forever.

That's why I admired Sissy Spacek.

She was a great actress who gave it up to raise her family.

Later she came back to do selective roles.

I'm not comparing myself to Sissy Spacek.

She was a much better actress than I could ever be.

But like her, what I want more than movie-stardom is love, children, animals, a contented home.

I think Jaro and I were moving toward that.

I will never understand why they killed my child.

They murdered Don Fernando then Kristin then Viktor.

They murdered me last.

The dark-haired one in the black leather miniskirt.

With the twisted mouth.

Swinging wildly, she stabbed me in the left shoulder.

Then, deliberately, she stabbed me in the belly.

Then I watched her do something mad. Incomprehensible.

She licked my baby's blood from the tip of her knife.

Then looked hard at me.

Then whispered in my ear, these, the last words I would hear on this sweet, sweet earth:

I'm the devil. I'm here to do devil's business.

Even the Devil—If there is a Devil—Had a Beginning

Jesus Coyote
(31 years after, shackled, Pelican State Prison)

Brought you your dentures.

Give 'em here, dog.

Back in Pelican Bay.

How many hard-ass joints I been in my life. Ain't nothing changed. No, no. Negativity, man. If I ask for a bucket of shit it's like: No fuckin' way, Coyote.

On your case.

[*laughs*] They'd ruther see me dead. 'Cept they afraid the fuckin' consequence. Still folks out there love my ass. If they don't love me, they need me, you dig? Most the other big-time devil soundbites are dead: Hitler, Che, Nixon, Jack the Ripper.

I'm what, 5-foot-3, 68-years-old, at world's end, shackled, sensory deprived, in supermax isolation, under 24/7 surveillance. Know why? I'm Jesus mo'fuckin' Coyote, evil incarnate, you dig?

5-3? I thought you were like 5-5.

Hard time shrinks a body.

First rape.

Bennett Home for Boys. Clarksburg, West Virginia. I was 10-years-old, youngest, smallest kid in the joint. Seven, eight bigger kids—they gang-raped me. When I got it together to go to the assistant superintendent, mo'fucker called Fish, he told me pull my pants down, bend over and show where they got me. When I did he spit tobacco juice on his hand and shoved it up my ass.

Then he says to the guard: "Okay, he's primed, let them fuck his brains out."

I never got a chance to even things up with Fish, but that night at about three a.m. I took a window crank—one them steel rods that push open or pull shut the windows. Was about 16 inches long and about three pounds. I went to the bunk of the first dude that fucked my ass and hit him eight or nine blows hard as I could hit to the head and face. About killed him. Too fuckin' bad I dint.

Father Flanagan's Boys Town.

Sent my ass there after I busted out of Bennett. But I busted out of Flanagan after like four days, me and some other kids. Stole cars and broke into stores an' shit. Held up one old guy and slapped him around a little bit. They caught us about four days later. Sent me to Prideaux Juvenile Detention in Indiana, which was raunchy. But I wasn't 'bout to do no time at no Father Mo'fucker's Boy's Town.

Death Valley.

Was love at first sight. Plus I'm a quick study. If I wasn't I wouldna made it this far.

Coyote.

Jesus crucified.

Watch a coyote move. He's rhythm and grace, aware of everything that's in motion because it's either prey or something gonna prey on him. You listen close for a long time to the coyote and you gonna hear just about every sound there is—howl, bark, growl, yip, wail, whistle. The coyote is total fear, total paranoia, which is what you must have to survive on this fucked-over planet. Yet he's relaxed, delicate in all his movements, at peace in his total fear that never ends. If a coyote is ever in trouble or captured he will do whatever it takes to get free, bite off his own tail or leg, even change identities, like become a sidewinder or a crow. That's why the Indians call him Trickster. If I wasn't a coyote I'd be a scorpion.

Rommel in the desert.

Rommel in the desert, Buddha in the desert, Jesus in the desert. I had all kinds of shit in mind one time or 'nother. You drop acid a bunch your mind gets to zoomin'. Mostly, I just wanted to be left alone with my coyotes and scorpions and geetar. I never made no big deal out of it. I was living in the desert. You all done come and git me, remember? I was happy doin' what I'm doin'.

Coyote tribe orgies on film.

[*laughs*] Yeah, we shot a lot of fim. And other humans—visitors and such—they shot us. We looked good and we knew how to fuck and suck. Everybody wanted a piece of us.

Some the fims we ourselves took we swapped for dope. The other fims—I know where they're at, dog, and they're hot. You get me sprung from Pelican Bay and you'll be doin' a whole lot of jackin' off to Coyote. [*laughs*]

Nature lover, vegetarian.

That's me. Just like Gandhi.

Just like Hitler.

I ain't got nuffin' 'gainst Hitler. Monster like me. That's what yawl made me. You fear me and you want to fuck me. Ain't that why you got all hotted up about the fims was shot of the tribe orgies?

Where the fims at, Coyote? How can I get my doggy paws on 'em? How can I slobber all over them with my forked tongue?

DA Leo Dickerson.

Wanted to gas Coyote and the tribe. He'd be right there in the execution chamber, first row, jackin' off in his head.

There I was on Death Row in Quentin kinda looking forward to the gas. But after that ACLU challenge went to the Supreme Court, they postponed, then commuted, all the pending executions. Had nothing to do with compassion, you dig? Was a legalism. This country of yours ain't into compassion for po' folks.

I didn't give a shit either way, but not executing Coyote broke Dickerson all up, I thought he was like to weep.

Beneath Dickerson's swagger he's a puss. In that lyin' book he got rich on, he has me so mojo powerful that just remembering one my stares would stop his pissing mid-flow.

The Coyote stare.

Simple, basic voodoo. Like me starin' at you now. You see how I'm starin' at you?

Answer me, dog.

I see.

Now you go home and try to fuck your wife, you ain't gon' be able. Just lookin' at you I can see your sex life wasn't worth shit to begin wit'. But I just wrecked what was left of it for all time.

I'm in supermax in Pelican Bay State Penitentiary, but I'm Coyote, right? So folks send me stuff, presents, neckties, socks, sweaters. I ain't no clothes horse and never was. Naked and dick swinging was my deal. So what I do with my hands cuffed is unravel the ties and socks and sweaters and tank tops and make voodoo dolls. I make scorpions and cockroach cages too.

[*laughs*] My dolls done murdered and maimed some bad-ass humans. You know as well as me some folks ain' fit to live.

God of fuck.

Dickerson made a big deal out of it. I said the god of fuck deal to Head Games first time I done her. Underneath a great old Redwood. Go ask Head Games how she liked it. Go ask all my other sweet-smelling girls. They was sweet-smelling back then.

Roxi Bakramp.

Shot off her mouth in jail. Sold some made-up story to one the weeklies.

Copped a plea before the grand jury. Became a quote-unquote born-again, but it still didn't get her ass sprung.

Before she joined up with the tribe she was a devil worshiper with what's his face up there in San Francisco. LaVey. Mindfuck was her thing. Whatever

Roxi was into Roxi wanted to be top dog, you dig? Fucking included. With me that never happened, you dig? After I balled her inside out and sideways, she done cried like a little girl. She'd go on 'bout how I was God. Which is dog spelled backwards.

Like some people, they say Roxi's gorgeous and sexy. Shit. Even the bulldykes in Frontera, where she's at, they won't go near her. She's toxic.

Bangkok Clap.

[*laughs*] That's a Roxi thang, right? If Roxi caught the clap she done caught it outside the tribe. She'd spread for anything that farted.

How many young folks moving through the tribe did I fuck? Thousand? Two thousand? Not a one of 'em ever had the Bangkok clap or the Timbuktu clap that I know of.

Haight-Ashbury.

It's 1967 and I just finished up 10 to 15 at Terminal Island, fed joint near San Pedro. I told 'em I didn't want to leave and they laughed at my ass. Bunch of murders and mayhem later [*laughs*], they wish they done kept my ass inside.

Takes me a little while get my shit together, then I thumb up to the Haight 'cuz that's where the cool runnings is at. I play my geetar, right? The fems jus' keep comin'. Marie Weston—she was a librarian at the University of San Francisco medical school. I was strummin' near Golden Gate Park, my black watch cap on the pavement for spare change. I see Marie Weston walking her boxer, dogshit bag in her hand, nose in the air, and I say real soft, "Babe, listen to this yere melody. I play it jus' for you." She stopped, I played the song. Bang.

Marie was the first. I called her Mercy and give her the color blue. Then came Head Games. I gave her the color green. Then came black-ass Roxi. Then LuAnn Hoy, who we called Ho, and Loca who was Daria Luz Shriver. And Bette Mulder.

It was getting crowded, you dig, so I scammed a school bus and painted it black. I named it Scorpion. We rode from the Haight up and down the coast, into Wyoming, Utah, Nevada, then back down to LA, pickin' up fems at ever' stop. Once in a while there'd be a dude.

Coyote does dudes.

Sho. I'm 68 years old and been in prison 56 years. Ain't no girls in prison that I know of.

Was one, pastor father of Lori-Kay Woerman, Worm we called her. She was like 14 when she got on the Scorpion outside of Flagstaff, I think it was. Well, by the time we got to LA her old man, Pentecostal pastor from Broken Arrow, Oklahoma, where Worm run away from—old man Woerman was waitin' on me with another dude, great big shaved-head mo'fucker packin' a semi-automatic. Desert Eagle 10-mm, if I remember correct.

No biggie. Problem solving is what I excel at, you dig? I sweet-talked them a little, fixed the shaved-head loon up with two my girls, then took a private walk with the preacher, slipped him some acid, and fucked him in the ass. You know that these Pentecostals talk in tongues, right? Well, this dude, Worm's old man out of Broken Arrow, Oklahoma, was squealin' in tongues while I was punkin' him. That's how much he loved my dick in his ass, you dig?

I dint feel the same way. Was like stickin' my fist in a sewer drain. After that, "Preacher" was one my most loyal followers. Till he died a year or so later.

Submit.

You and honkies like you cain't see that these hundreds of young humans that joined my tribe were humans that you all abandoned, humans alongside the road that, when they wouldn't eat their cheeseburgers, their parents kicked them out or tried to stick them in Juvenile Hall. So I done the Christian thing and took them in and told them that in love there was no wrong. All they had to do was give up the lies and bad shit they learned and submit. Submission.

Anger and rage.

My ma dropped me when she was 15 and a ho 'cuz she was an illiterate Appalachian hillbilly. I never knew my pop. We scrambled from town to town. I done 7 years for a 37 dollar check. I done 12 years because I was piss-poor without no parents. I was gang-raped in reform school when I was 10-years-old. Yeah I had anger and rage.

How's anyone not going to have anger and rage living in what they done turned this sweet world into?

Devil's hole in Death Valley.

What was down the hole it ain't for foo's like you all to know. But I'll say this. I found a hole that goes down to a river that runs north underground. I called it a bottomless pit because where could a river be flowing north underground? Was so wide and deep you could even sail a ship on it. Wasn't no penal institutions and TV down there. So I covered it up and called it "The Devil's Hole."

Black folks.

Ever since I offed that 300 pound wannabe Black Panther spade Lotsapoppa in self-defense in '68, I think it was, people, even so-called Coyote experts, been sayin' I have trouble with blacks and such, but it ain't no truth to it. Like Lamar Duane Cady, we called him Fang, the Skull Helmet biker that lived on the movie ranch, he hated blacks, and when he'd rap with me I'd like nod my head. So he'd go away sayin': Coyote agrees with me. But I was just reflectin' back what he hisself thought.

Yo, I been in prison all my life, and that's the first thing you learn: go wit' the flow 'less you're big enough and shit-eating enough to bust some heads. See, I ain't big, but I'm shit-eating.

You know what else? I'm a piss-poor hillbilly spend all my fuckin' life in prison. Prisons in damn near every city in this country of yours. And who's in these prisons? Black folks and po' folks. A piss-poor hillbilly in the joint ain' nuffin' but a nigger.

Reflecting back.

What I'm reflectin' back is this country we live in. Hypocrisy, lust in the head, xenophobia, cruelty to your brother. It ain't that I am or do these things, you dig, but that people—family people like you all—see in me what's in their deepest selves but that they cain't bear to look at. That's why for so long I was the most famous face in all of capitalism.

Dr. Pepper.

My ma's younger brother was named Luther Kinlock. He lived in West Virginia, which is where we moved from Ohio when I was not even a year old. Luther didn't have no kind of real job so him and Kathleen—my ma—they decided to rob a gas station in Charleston, West Virginia. What they used as a weapon was a full bottle of Dr. Pepper which they tried to hit the attendant on the head with, but they messed up and got nabbed.

Pimp Coyote.

Older con that ran wit' Bonnie and Clyde—he told me once there was nothing like turning a fem out. He was on the money. Deep down every fem wants to be a ho. I was real good at seeing they got what they wanted. And it bought me time to set around, get stoned, do my music.

Punked in Quentin.

'Nother lie makin' the rounds, that some Aryan Brotherhood dude made me his bitch when I was in Quentin in the Seventies. Nobody done touched me inside since that time I was gang-raped as a kid. Well, this Pachuco gang doused me with paint thinner and lit me up. That was in Calipatria, by the border. I got some my hair and skin burned. No big deal. And three skanky Hare Krishna cons jumped me, but that was in Soledad. I kicked their asses all over the yard, the three of 'em.

The Krishnas thought I was dissing their Hindu jive. With the Mex gang it was Macho. Light Coyote up and get famous.

Cocksman.

[*laughs*] You lookin' at him.

Lotta folks ask me who was better, me or Cupid, Billy San-Soleil.

Lovin' good takes a good dick, but that ain't all. It's like the way innocent little kids play, every bit of the body alive. Me, I fired from all cylinders. At the same time I always took my time, knew just what the fem wanted. And I gave it to her. Just not all at once, you dig?

Yeah, the tribe girls loved Cupid's dick, and he knew how to use it. But after I copped him in the ass I owned him. He'd do anything I say.

Jaroslav Hora.

Polish ham.

You shattered his life.

Man, I don't give a fuck about no Polish ham.

Will you outlive Hora? You're the same age and size. Five-foot-three inch cocks of the walk. Big-time dopers and fuck machines in your prime. He made movies about gory murders. You did it in real time.

Live, outlive. Don't mean nuffin' to me. I shit ever' day and make my voodoo dolls for one reason—Mo'fuckers like you all ruther see my ass dead.

You're staying alive to spite your enemies.

Das righ'.

Dennis Wilson of the Beach Boys.

I was waitin' on him at his fancy house, it was like 3:30 a.m. As he pulled into the driveway in his Ferrari, I stepped out of the shadows. Dude saw me and was like: Please don't hurt me. I said: Do I look like I'm going to hurt you, brother? And I never did hurt him neither. Though sometimes he gave me cause. He copped my music, stuck it on one of his LP's, changed a few my lyrics and never gave me no credit for it.

Two-and-a-half incandescent years...

I know where you're goin'. We done a lifetime load of bad shit in that short time, right?

So if I was offered a devil's bargain: two-and-a-half years, like what I had with my girls and sex and dope and Death Valley and those raunchy murders that I supposedly done or instigated—if I was offered them two-and-a-half years in exchange for spending the rest of my life in prison, would I take it?

You know what, it took me a while to get in the groove. After doin' 13 in Terminal Island I was on the streets a lot of days before I got my nuts out of hock. Once I found the groove, though, it done never stopped like you said. And I ain't gonna lie to you: I enjoyed the ride.

'Cept close to the end, around the time the big murders—'cuz there was some other murders folks still don't know about—close to the end, the shit turned. Was me callin' the shots and I let us slip into this end-of-the-world thing, diggin' up bunkers, storing water and supplies, keepin' a step ahead the pigs that was out to nail us.

Tribe would look at me like, "What now, Soul?" And I wasn't always able to tell' 'em. My creativity was slipping. I guess it was that two-and-a-half year devil's pact comin' to an end.

But would I do it again, even if I knew on one side was prison and on the other side was prison? Yeah, I would. Because prison ain't that big a deal, dog. Jail sucks but it's my home.

Helter Skelter?

Was a goof. Bunch of us on the movie ranch was stoned on acid and jivin' around. Someone, maybe Bitch, come up with that old Beatles White Album, and we got to listenin' to it close, with the acid workin'. We started messin' with the coded lyrics an' shit, and we pulled out race war.

Man, I could care less about the fuckin' White Album. I'm a hillbilly. Gimme Woody Guthrie. Gimme Hank Williams senior. Gimme early Dylan on acoustic.

The Naomi Self massacre.

Wasn't me that done her, dog. I didn't know her or the Polish ham that was her husband 'cuz I never did see none their flicks. Yeah, I hung out a little with actors and shit, and this one famous matinee idol—he's dead now and I won't say his name—paid me to fuck his ass. But I never mixed with no Naomi Self.

Freaky shit, I like it.

Roxi said that when she tasted the blood off the knife she used to stab Naomi Self in her pregnant belly. Roxi admitted it then denied it. But Tex Embry and Chong both heard her say it.

Jesus Christ.

You a church-going human so maybe you know that before the church fathers got ahold of him, Jesus was a Essene, a hippy. He wore a jellaba, which is a long robe, with no underwear, not even a jock strap. What a family man like you would call an athletic supporter. He had long hair, and traveled with a bunch of long-haired followers. Apostles he called them. Ring a bell?

Coyote and his soul-tribe.

You ain't such a dumb mangy dog as you look, dog.

Dig it: You 5-foot-3 and in hard-ass penal institutions your whole damn life you learn to adjust or else you die. You puff up like Mike Tyson, you squeeze and shrink and fade like road kill, you vibe out like Jesus…

You got to understand just a little bit of this without my sayin'. Man, I sometimes wish they'd send me someone has some brain and maybe just a little bit of soul. But I reckon ain't too many like that out there. See, what you and your kind are is just what we was fightin' 'gainst back then. Rid the fuckin' earth of yawl.

You lost that fight.

Wrong again. What you all think is lost has just gone underground. Like a desert plant, you dig? Could take another 10, 20 years for the right conditions then it will rise again faster than you can believe, all strong and prickly. Foo' like you put his hand on it come away poisoned and bloody.

Favorite mass-murderer excluding yourself.

Finally you come up wit' a question that ain't half-ass. Favorite mass-murderer excluding myse'f?

That would be Henry Kissinger. Madonna called him Caca. She was fuckin' him. You remember OJ, right? The Juice? Well, OJ'd bang Madonna from behind while she doin' a strap-on number on Caca. Sometimes she'd ram her fist up there. He liked it. Caca. His stretch limo be waitin' outside.

Took place in Madonna's Park Avenue triplex. Was a regular occurrence Madonna, OJ, Caca. This was way before the OJ trial.

I sometimes think what if I had slick Johnny Cochran argue *my* case. Know what? I woulda walked. I'd be back in the desert with the coyotes and scorpions fingerin' my geetar.

Provisional final words.

Yo, I had my run. Two-and-a-half incandescent years. Ain't that the word you used: incandescent? Now I'm back inside where I belong. Ever'body has to have some kinda home. Pelican Bay. Don't it have a nice sound? You know what I do in my supermax isolation cell in Pelican Bay? I sit there thinking of nothing. Nothing to think about. If I could, I'd jerk this microphone out and beat your brains out with it, because that's what you and the rest yawl deserve. But I don't have none that anger and rage you was talkin' about. You're a scabby, housebroken old dog. A dumb, soulless motherfuckin' piece of shit wears a nametag and do just what they want you to do. You know how quick I could slit your belly, snatch out your liver? But do I want to get your pissy blood all over me? No, I don't. I most definitely don't. I'm just settin' here wit' my shackled hands pickin' my imaginary geetar waitin' on some ties and socks and tee shirts so that I can make voodoo dolls for all the upstanding Christian human beans out there in Freedomland.

Works Cited

Roxi

Susan Atkins, *Child of Satan, Child of God* (Logos International, 1977), p. 71.

Head Games

*Jess Bravin, *Squeaky: The Life and Times of Lynette Alice Fromme*, pp. 72-75. (Buzz Books, 1997).

** Bravin, 58.

About the Author

Harold Jaffe is the author of ten fiction (or "docufiction") collections, three novels, and a collection of creative nonfiction. Titles include: *Beasts*, *Eros Anti-Eros*, *Terror-dot-Gov*, *Straight Razor, Madonna and Other Spectacles, Sex for the Millennium, 15 Serial Killers, Mourning Crazy Horse, Jesus Coyote, Beyond the Techno-Cave: A Guerrilla Writer's Guide to Post-Millennial Fiction.*

His fiction and creative nonfiction have been anthologized in *Pushcart Prize, Best American Stories, Best of American Humor, Storming the Reality Studio, American Made, Avant Pop: Fiction for a Daydreaming Nation, After Yesterday's Crash, and* elsewhere. His writings have been translated into German, Japanese, Spanish, Italian, French, Polish, and Czech. He has won two National Endowment awards in fiction, a California Arts Council grant in fiction, a New York State CAPS grant in fiction, and two Fulbright grants: to India and to Prague.

Jaffe is editor-in-chief of *Fiction International* and Professor of Literature and Creative Writing at San Diego State University.

Other Novels from Raw Dog Screaming Press

Blankety Blank, D. Harlan Wilson
hc 978-1-933293-50-9, $14.95, 188p
tpb 978-1-933293-57-8, $29.95, 188p

Rutger Van Trout has problems but the worst is not that his son might be a werewolf. It's not his obsession with transforming his house into a three-ring barnyard or his wife's haunted skeleton. The complication has invaded his community in the form of a new breed of serial killer, who stalks from house to house leaving a bloodbath that would make Jack the Ripper himself blush.

Isabel Burning, Donna Lynch
hc 978-1-933293-49-3, $29.95, 236p
tpb 978-1-933293-56-1, $15.95, 236p

Isabel's new job as housekeeper at Grace mansion allows her to observe the habits of the enigmatic Dr. Edward Grace. Captivated by his tales of travel to Africa, she is inexorably drawn into a tumultuous relationship which eventually reveals the Grace family's dark heritage and lays bare every secret, even the ones she keeps from herself.

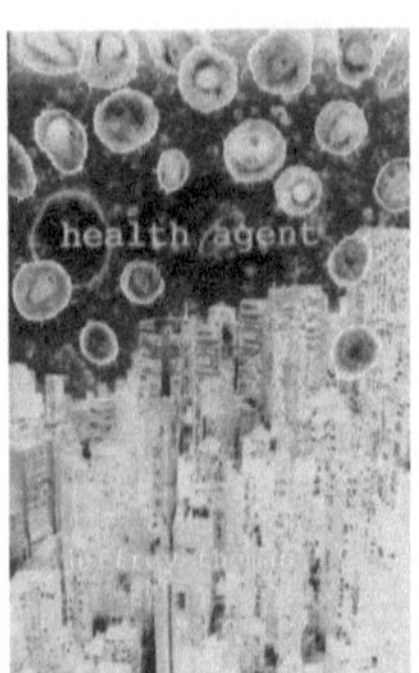

Health Agent, Jeffrey Thomas
hc 978-1-933293-43-1, $30.00, 290p
tpb 978-1-933293-44-8, $15.95, 290p

Punktown's health agents are keep the public safe from infectious disease. But work is about to consume Montgomery Black's life. The problem is a highly contagious and extremely deadly STD, mutstav six-seventy. While trying to prevent the spread of the disease Black could lose everything he cares about but there's no ignoring the suspicion that something far more sinister than the impartial hand of nature is behind the spread of this epidemic.

Sin Conductor, John Edward Lawson
tpb 978-1-933293-65-3

Willis Lowery is just your average occupational hazards estimator until one day, while inspecting a factory, he happens across a chemical burn victim. Her name is Dusyanna, and the passion she ignites in him threatens to melt away every fiber of his morals. As he soon learns, there is no escape from her circle of degenerates, so he vows to become the devil to beat the devil.

www.rawdogscreaming.com

www.ingramcontent.com/pod-product-compliance
Lightning Source LLC
Chambersburg PA
CBHW050821180626
46814CB00004B/1400

* 9 7 8 1 9 3 3 2 9 3 6 3 9 *